Caithness Writers

DREAMS

Written, edited, proofread, and published
by members of Caithness Writers

Other Publications by Caithness Writers

Anthology of Caithness Crime Stories
Beyond the Mist
Flights of Imagination
Stacks
Connections

Copyright © 2021 Caithness Writers

The moral rights of the authors have been asserted.

Apart from any fair dealing for the purposes of research or private study, or criticism or review, as permitted under the Copyright, Design and Patents Act, 1988, this publication may only be reproduced, stored or transmitted, in any form or by any means, with the prior permission in writing of the publishers, or in the case of photographic reproduction in accordance with the terms of licences issued by the Copyright Licencing Agency. Enquiries concerning reproduction outside those terms should be sent to the publishers.

This is a work of fiction and, except in the case of historical fact, any similarity to persons who may have existed is merely coincidental.

https://www.facebook.com/Caithness-Writers-536106093071994

Published by
Overtheord Publishing
8-10 Louisburgh Street
Wick KW1 4BY

Sinclair and Girnigoe Castle

Contents

DREAMS 1
by Meg Macleod 1

FLYING GEESE 2
by Sharon Gunason Pottinger 2

CATASTROPHE 9
by Jean McLennan 9

THE WOLF CLAN 13
by Meg MacLeod 13

ADDICTION 14
by Morag Anderson 14

BEGGARS CAN BE CHOOSERS 16
by Margaret Wood 16

BUTTERFLIES 20
by Meg Macleod 20

LEGACY 21
by J. L Brook 21

BLITZ	33
by Margaret Mackay	33
ALTNABREAC	37
by John Knowles	37
A WALK AT TWILIGHT	51
by Sharon Gunason Pottinger	51
THE WITCH ON THE CLIFF	53
by Catherine Byrne	53
TO TELL OR NOT TO TELL	67
by Morag Anderson	67
A STICK TO BEAT MY MOTHER	70
by John Crofts	70
ACCORDION AFTERNOON	76
by Sharon Gunason Pottinger	76
HARBOUR LIGHTS	77
by Jean MacLennan	77
THE RIVER BANK	83
by Irena Bracey	83

MY VOICE **89**
by Meg Macleod 89

WHAT IS REALITY **90**
by Alan Sinclair 90

SAVING THE SEALS **103**
by Catherine M Byrne 103

A DIFFERENT BALL GAME **111**
by Margaret Wood... 111

CURSE OF THE CAITHNESS ZUAICH... **117**
by John Knowles 117

Dreams

by Meg Macleod

A flutter of winged darkness
Who goes there?
What sound?

All manner of fears emerge
Twining into words

with the rising of the sun

Flying Geese

by Sharon Gunason Pottinger

Her mother was excited. 'Today your father is going to fly.'

'Does he have wings?'

Her mother laughed her happy laugh. Eilidh hadn't heard that laugh since they'd moved into their new house. 'No, love, in an aeroplane. You'll have heard them flying overhead.'

Eilidh nodded as her mother turned off the main road. 'Keep hold of my hand because we're not supposed to be here, but we can see your father from here.'

'In the sky?'

'Yes.' Clutching Eilidh's hand in hers, she hurried to the edge of a building with a large door ajar. We'll wait in here 'til we hear the engines start, then we'll go out to watch.'

Hamish sighed at the sight of the telegram. He'd delivered too many in the war. Perhaps, just perhaps, now the war was done, it would be good news. It was addressed to Margaret Henderson. He'd been dropping in for a cuppa at the end of his route since her sister Shona and the bairn, Eilidh, had left. He parked his little red van in the usual spot and called out, 'Put the kettle on, I've a thirst from all these letters.' If he kept to the routine, then everything would be fine he told himself.

'Aye, and no doubt hungry, too,' Margaret said, coming to the door. She stopped as she saw the telegram in his hand.

Hamish helped her to a seat. 'I'll bring you tea with lots of sugar.'

'Training exercise,' she said, when Hamish came back with the tea. 'Killed. I must come and collect the bairn. Why should they die now? The war is over.'

'There's never any sense to it. Drink your tea,' he said, wrapping her hands around the warm mug.

She seemed not to have moved from the chair as the world whirled around her. The minister stopped by. Someone brought her a suitcase and a doll for Eilidh. Margaret put the doll on top of the coverlet she'd been making for Eilidh. She had thought she and Shona would finish it together.

Hamish drove her in the post van to the train station. She'd never been further than Inverness. Had never wanted to, and now she was off to Germany to collect her niece. There were people to help her at the airport and from the airport to the hospital. She identified her sister in the mortuary. She hoped the sight of her sister, small and pale and damaged would not linger, but she was struggling to recall Shona's face as it had been.

'And now, if you're all right,' the young woman said, not unkindly but detached, 'I'll take you to your niece.'

Eilidh, too, looked diminished. Children should be like lambs always moving or about to move. Her legs hung over the edge of the chair, not quite reaching the floor. They were so still that Margaret thought she was hurt, too. The woman sensed this. 'She's all right—considering. She had a slight concussion and a bit of temporary hearing loss, but we think she'll be all right.'

'You *think*?'

'I'll get the doctor to speak with you,' she said and she was gone. Margaret wanted to scoop Eilidh into her arms and say that none of this had happened, but she looked like a porcelain figurine that the slightest touch might damage beyond repair. Margaret stood there, 'Eilidh?' she called softly.

Eilidh turned to her with a face pale and tight. 'Mother said I need to go to Aunt Margaret, but I don't know the way.'

'Don't worry, love. I'm here, I came for you. Look, here's a photo to help you remember—there's you and your mother and father and me. That was taken just before you left.'

Eilidh clutched the photo to her chest, her head dropped, and she was sleeping like a small bird making its own nest.

Margaret swallowed her own sobs, but small hot tears rolled down her face. She swiped them hastily away as the doctor came in.

'Please sit. You probably want to know what happened?'

'I need to know,' Margaret said.

The doctor understood the difference between *needing* and *wanting*, and so began mentally editing. He sighed, picked up a pipe, looked at her as if to ask, do you mind, and began. 'There was an accident. One plane caught the wing of another one. They are investigating what happened, but that does not affect you except to know that your brother-in-law was fatally wounded. Some debris from the collision fell to the ground near where your sister and the little one were standing. Your sister, I am sorry to say, died when she was struck by something off the plane.'

He paused and looked up at Margaret. Some people want to know if their loved one suffered or details of their death. He was relieved to see that Margaret appeared not to want details. 'Either the force of the explosion or your sister pushed the little one out of the way. Eilidh was relatively protected. The concussion and the temporary hearing loss should not be a worry. I'll give you a report to take to your surgery. The biggest concern is what appears to be elective mutism.'

'She spoke to me,' Margaret said, as if that had broken the spell of the silence.

'That's encouraging. It may be a selective mutism, in which a child can speak to some people or not to others. As you noted, she spoke to you—but something has her locked up so tightly inside she cannot speak, at least not in the way I'm assuming she used to.'

'What am I to do?' Margaret said, thinking not only of the

mutism but also everything else that she didn't even have names for.

'Time,' the doctor said, spreading his hands out like a magician showing he had nothing up his sleeve. 'Time,' he repeated, laying his hands flat on his desk. There was no magic; no more words to be offered up. He stood, 'Unless you have more questions…'

The same woman who had spoken to her earlier took them back to the airport. On the plane home, Margaret recalled the days before Shona left. Margaret loved quilting with the wives of the American soldiers stationed at Forss, especially the names of the quilt patterns and the stories behind them: Log Cabin, wedding rings, star of Bethlehem. Each one had variations as unique as the quilter. Shona liked the quilting when they all got together. It was there that Shona met Thomas. Perhaps if she'd not taken Shona, perhaps… Margaret looked at the tiny form beside her. Eilidh slept curled into a ball still clutching the photograph. If not for the quilting, this wee one would not be here and that was all that mattered now.

On the train ride home, Eilidh looked out the window and slept. She did what was asked of her, but offered no more conversation since those first words. Margaret thought the sight of the house she had known might spark something, but Eilidh was silent then and in the weeks that followed, more than wordless, even her footsteps were quiet. She went to school and did as she was told until she had to recite in front of the class. She stood there silent with such anguish that the teacher, Mr Drever, who could be severe, leaned over to Eilidh and said, gently. 'I am not angry with you. I want the best for you. Do you understand?' Eilidh nodded. For a moment it looked as if she might say something, but she cried quietly.

Margaret came to school to collect her. Her small frame looked as forlorn as that first day. 'Let's go for a walk. I'll show you where your mother and I used to play up on the hill at the peat banks.' Eilidh slipped her hand into hers. The day was warm for September, and the sky was such a blue you could imagine it was the dome of heaven.

Eilidh climbed to the top of a small hill looking over the land as if she knew she belonged there, her legs already covered in the fine brown-black dust of the peats. The wind picked up and began to switch her skirt around her knees. Eilidh turned into the wind, spread her arms, and laughed as it tousled her hair. Both Margaret and Eilidh heard them before they saw them: a skein of geese flying from the Arctic to the relative warmth of Caithness. Margaret saw them as determined specks in a wedge slicing through the blue sky, a marker of a change in season.

Eilidh looked up, alarmed by the geese flying overhead. She put her hands over her ears and began screaming shrill and desperate, ringing out like a siren. She collapsed and began rolling down the hill, covering herself in the colour of the landscape. by the time Margaret reached her, the screaming had become raspy sobs and gasps. 'It was my fault. All my fault. Mother said to hold tight. I let go, and they fell out of the sky. It's all my fault,' she said and then she went limp.

Margaret picked her up and began running awkwardly toward the house. Hamish saw her lumbering toward the house and ran across the field to meet them. He took Eilidh in his arms and carried her into the house. Margaret came along panting with the exertion and the shock.

'I'll get the nurse,' Hamish said, jumping into his van. 'You see to the little one.'

Margaret chaffed Eilidh's hands and cooed and spoke to her, 'It's not your fault. It's not your fault. Oh, my little lamb, it's not your fault. Wake up, love. Look at me. Your mother loved you so much. The last thing she did was push you away—she pushed you away to save you. It's hard to explain, but when you are loved as much as your mother loved you, you will leave everything else behind. I finally understand. Do you hear me, Eilidh? Oh please come back. I can't lose you, too.'

Hamish sat with Margaret while the nurse examined Eilidh. She came out smiling. 'Everything is normal—temperature, pressure. I'm not an expert, but she may have screamed herself back into the world, like a newborn again.'

Words came back to Eilidh slowly at first and then like a burn in spate.

More than two years after the day on the peats, Shona's trunk arrived from Germany. Margaret stared at it. Should she put it in the loft unopened? She could not bear losing Eilidh again to the stillness, and her own grief was still too fresh. Before she could decide, Eilidh burst into the house and nearly tumbled over the trunk. 'I recognise that,' she said.

Margaret could not read the emotion in her voice. 'We can put it up in the loft if you'd rather not…'

Eilidh walked around it wordlessly. She ran her fingers over the top. Finally, she looked up at Margaret. 'I don't think there's anything in there that can hurt us now.'

The lock was broken, but the latches were stiff with rust. It took time and effort to open the lid. 'Margaret sat back on her heels when the lid was finally raised. There on the top was the quilt she had made for Shona. She felt again the joy of seeing Shona happy and the pain of losing her.

'I remember this,' Eilidh said, running her hand along the topstitching. I liked to trace the patterns.

'It's called wedding rings,' Margaret said. 'I made it for your mother when she and your father got married.'

'I know she loved it; I didn't know it had a name.'

'All the quilt patterns have names. I can show you in my books.'

Together they hung the quilt on the line to air it. 'Tonight we'll wrap you in this, so you can dream of your mother.'

Eilidh spent hours studying the patterns in Margaret's books. She was quiet again, but a different silence from the sad days.

'Can we make one?' she asked one night after dinner.

'Yes, but it's a big job. When it comes time to back it and quilt it, we'll need to get some help. Your mother was good at that.'

'Did she like looking at the designs?'

'Not as much as you do. Have you found something in my books for your quilt?

'Yes,' Eilidh said, smiling broadly. 'I liked the shape—the big v with the little ones behind it. When I saw the name, I knew it was what I wanted,' she said holding out the book and pointing.

Margaret put down the dish towel and came to look at the page. 'Flying geese?' Margaret said caught between a laugh and a cry.

Eilidh laughed. 'What else? 'On the front, pale blue—like a summer sky.'

'And the geese—the triangles?' Margaret began.

'I'd like to make the triangles all different—same but different. We can use pieces of my old dresses—even some of my mother's maybe?'

Catastrophe

by Jean McLennan

His plate should have been full of Felix, but as Tiger arrived it was to see the departing behind of Bailey, the labradoodle with whom he shared his home. The dog turned, licking his lips, and Tiger could swear he was grinning. A smell from the kitchen counter called out to his empty belly and with no human in the room, he took a chance. Just as the morsel of cheese was within his grasp, Mrs McTavish returned. 'Shoo,' she said, shaking a tea towel in his direction. Worse was to come later that evening when he was unceremoniously dumped outside just as a downpour was getting underway. The lady of the house wagged an empty Dreamies packet at him.

'Back at opening cupboards, eh? We'll see about that.'

He was entirely innocent of the charge and knew exactly who had polished off his treats. Bailey was pushing his luck. He made a plan to get even. Next day he put it into action.

'Meow. Attention all.' Tiger was the self-appointed leader of all the local cats, as the biggest. He surveyed the felines arranged around him. Suki, a black Persian with luxuriant, high-maintenance fur, was, as usual, washing her paws. Socks' whiskers trembled in a small growl while he salivated watching a fat pigeon teetering on a branch nearby. Texas, (where did that name come from—humans, inexplicable!), a torn-eared grey whose main claim to fame was most projectiles had been aimed at him for nocturnal carousing. Nearby, Smokey, another grey, British Blue pedigree he claimed, was eyeing up all the females speculating about which might be mother to his next brood. The others were snoozing in various, comfortable places where the sun warmed their fur.

'Meeeeooow, meeting come to order,' Tiger commanded. 'Listen carefully.' He was pleased to see, for a moment at least, he seemed to have everyone's attention.

'We need to do something about Bailey and the other dogs that live among us. Do you agree?'

There was a general murmur of approval. He recounted the events of the previous evening shuddering at the recollection. He'd been hungry all night.

'Guess who got the blame?' Suki nodded her head at this. Tiger had previous. He'd developed a skill of opening cupboards and even the fridge which now boasted a special lock. She witnessed Mrs McTavish say it was cat-proof and Tiger saying, 'We'll see.'

'I'm sick of being chased out of my own garden,' Texas piped up.

'If that Honey takes up the whole of the fireside rug again...' added Suki. There were general mutterings of all the sins the dog population of the area had perpetrated.

'So what are we going to do?' asked Smokey, treating Tiddles, a young tabby, to a saucy look and a flick of his tail. She might just be the one.

'I was just coming to that,' growled Tiger. 'We'll hit them where it hurts. All dogs love dog chocolate, don't they?' he paused but didn't wait for an answer. It was self-evident. Dogs would eat anything, given a chance, but dog chocolate seemed as good to them as a tasty sardine would be to him. 'There's only one place that sells it here and I heard on the grapevine new stock will be arriving this afternoon. I think we should steal it.'

'Will they not just eat something else?' asked Socks.

'True,' Tiger responded but he had hopes of a bigger picture, one he wasn't about to share just yet. 'So,' he stood up, stretched and looked imperiously at the others, 'Here's the plan.'

When the lorry arrived Suki crawled into *Pets at Home* on her belly yowling. It was a convincing act. The staff love their animals and, even leaving customers in the queue unattended, they totally focussed on getting help for the apparently ailing cat. The dog chocs were spirited off the lorry and into the bin store at the delivery entrance to be removed and carried in convoy later to a treehouse in the McTavish garden, perfectly accessible to a cat but impossible for any dog.

'Sorry, Bailey,' said Mrs McTavish, *Pets at Home* had no dog chocs this week.' Every week when she did her shopping he got a few treats when she arrived home. 'You'll have to do without. it'll be at least next Friday before they get any more. The dog's shoulders slumped and he sloped off to throw himself down on his bed.

'See what it feels like now?' asked Tiger. 'When you stole my treats and I got the blame?'

Bailey raised his head, cocked his ears.

'Do you know something about this?' he growled.

'Yep. And there won't be any on Friday either unless you stop all this nonsense. You and all the other dogs around here. We cats are sick of it.'

'So what do you want?'

Tiger laid out his and his friends' requirements. No stealing cat food or treats, no hogging the best, warmest places on a cool night, no chasing and no misbehaviour for which a cat might be blamed.

Bailey undertook to run it past his friends on his next walk and on his return said agreement had been reached.

The dog chocs were recovered from under the tree house and carried back to the delivery entrance of the pet store. Bailey asked if he might have some but Tiger told him that he would probably gorge on them and make himself ill. He remembered inadvertently stepping in the result when Bailey had helped himself to a largely untouched takeaway that had been lobbed over the McTavish garden wall. Never again.

Mrs McTavish was astounded when she returned from the WRI a couple of days later to find Bailey and Tiger lying side by side in front of the fire. The cats met and reported that the truce was holding and everyone seemed to be happy.

That was until a new Rottweiler puppy, Buster, arrived who didn't know the rules and who chased every cat in the neighbourhood, claimed the best places in his home putting two cats' noses out of joint and eating everything he could including fat pigeons. As he grew, which he did quickly, he was soon the biggest dog in the neighbourhood and the other dogs did his bidding. Buster rewrote the rule book. Tiger sighed. They were back to the bad old days. He needed a new plan.

The Wolf Clan

by Meg MacLeod

today the matriarch and the youngling
became wolf clan

we raised our voices to the half moon
the freedom of our howling
dissolving the years between us

we laughed
let's do that again we said
and we howled our way
into a wilderness harmony

Addiction

by Morag Anderson

What rubbish, it was only one too many, being sociable, she told herself. She always wanted to be sociable. It started with the half bottle in her handbag, the little pick-me-up before a meeting, the dutch courage to smooth the bumps in life, not a problem, no, of course not, she did *not* have a problem.

Yes, it was only being sociable. Dan, her husband had decided not to be sociable anymore but that was unimportant. The authorities had taken the children, but that didn't matter, she had a much more compelling reason for living. The house. She didn't really want to stay there anymore anyway, and as for her job, does the world need another lawyer?

It was nice in the park, she had her own private bench hidden in the trees, she had her own toilet for washing and she had friends, sociable friends.

Rainy days were not the best. The shelter often turned her away. Sometimes she was just too sociable to be admitted. But they were good Christians, only wanted the best for her, so they said. She did not understand their god, this god they worshipped, this god that would make her happy. She had her own god, whom she worshipped every day. He made her feel happy.

She had her ways, she had her favourite spots, she knew how to look vulnerable and evoke pity. She had her regular 'customers' as she liked to think of them. The man who, once a week, dropped five one-pound coins in her hat saying, as always, 'Don't spend this on drink, get yourself some food.'

Of course, she thought, *what else would she do with it?* The young girl in the office across the street often made herself too much lunch. 'Here,' she would say, 'you have this,' handing her a sandwich of one sort or another. She never went hungry. There were always the bins; she knew them all. No one ever finished their Chinese carry-out.

Did she ever regret it? No. She had everything she ever wanted; it came in a bottle. It would never run out, there was always another bottle where that one came from.

Haven't seen Mavis for a couple of weeks thought the man as he returned the coins to his pocket. *Haven't seen Mavis for a while,* thought the girl from the office, eating her extra sandwich.

It was the dog, attracted by the smell in the end. Two weeks under a park bench.

Dan, her husband, was a charming man, always attentive and caring, They had lived in a nice new house with their three little girls. Mavis had worked hard to get on in life.

'Pull yourself together,' her friends would say. And she had tried.

'It is a disease,' they said. 'Anyone can catch it,' they said.

R.I.P Mavis, sociable to the end.

Beggars Can be Choosers

by Margaret Wood

Lil folded her newspaper and stowed it into the rucksack on the pavement beside her. The commuter rush would start in a few moments and they might think twice about dropping money into her tin if they saw her reading *The Racing Post*. She settled herself in a more comfortable position on her blanket and leaned back against the warm stonework of the wall. It was going to be another hot day. Thank goodness she'd found this cotton dress in the charity shop.

'A real bargain,' the woman had said. 'Why don't you try it on?'

Lil had been reluctant. She avoided mirrors as much as possible. She couldn't get used to the image that stared back at her: the unkempt hair, the face free of any care or cosmetic, the ragbag of clothes.

'It'll be fine,' she said, but the woman persisted.

'Try it on. We can't take it back later. I wouldn't want you to waste your money.'

Lil nearly laughed out loud when she thought of the money that had drained through her fingers in the past. But the woman was trying to be kind.

'Come out and give us a twirl, ducks,' she'd called through

the fitting-room curtain.

So Lil had paraded in the gaudy floral.

'Not bad, not bad at all,' said the woman. 'Though you could have done with a size smaller. Still, beggars can't....'

Her voice trailed away and colour flooded her cheeks as she realised what she had said. Lil felt her own face burn and she fled to the privacy of the changing room. But, looking on the bright side, the woman did knock a pound off the price.

The sound of money hitting metal brought her back to the present.

'Thanks,' she called after the young woman who was hurrying away as though trying to distance herself from her generous impulse.

And then she saw him. Simon Lorimer. The love of her life. At least he had been twenty years earlier when they were students. He was standing outside the station, gazing around as though searching for someone. Hopefully not that awful Juliet Maxwell that he'd married. Lil couldn't bear for them to see her like this. She ducked her head and shrank back against the wall.

'Excuse me.'

That voice. Only two words, but she could tell it hadn't changed — still dark and smooth as melted chocolate, still sending shivers down her spine. She looked up praying that he wouldn't recognise her.

'Yes?'

He smiled and that hadn't changed either, although his body was bulkier and the black hair that she had loved to run her fingers through was now flecked with grey. He wore the dark suit and crisp shirt of a successful businessman.

'You seem to be the only person not dashing about,' he said. 'Can you tell me the way to Moor Street?'

'Sure.' She turned away from him. 'Cross here. Then take the first on the right....'

'You're Lilian Greig.'

She could hear the disbelief in his voice and was grateful for it. It was nice to know that he hadn't expected her to end up as a bag lady. She faced him square on.

'That's right. And you're Simon Lorimer.'

Now she could see the pity etched on his face. Those gorgeous brown eyes were full of it and she couldn't stand it.

'Look, Simon, it's not what it seems. I actually work for a TV company and we're doing a documentary about homelessness. I'm what you might call undercover at the moment. So be a love and don't give me away. I'm not supposed to tell anybody and the producer would go mad if she knew.'

'Oh, Lord,' he said. 'I suppose there's a hidden camera somewhere.'

'Yeah, somewhere. They don't tell me where. So just let me point you in the direction of Moor Street and I can go back to being the beggar maid.'

She could feel his eyes on her as she pointed out the direction he should take.

'Thanks,' he said when she finished. 'You know, I hate seeing you like this, even if it is all pretence. Why don't we get together when your programme is over? It would be great to catch up. I've just moved to this area. I'll be using this station every day so if you know somewhere hereabouts where we could have a drink, it would be great.' He took out his wallet and handed her a card. 'My phone number. Do ring.' He smiled that heart-stopping smile again. 'Now I'd better let you get back in character.'

She watched him take a few paces away. Then he stopped and turned back.

'Nearly forgot.' Grinning, he fished a coin from his pocket and dropped it into her tin. It was two pounds. 'In the interests of authenticity,' he said. Then he winked and was gone.

Lil didn't know whether to laugh or cry. She took the coin from the tin and pressed it against her cheek. She imagined that it was still warm from his contact. In an ideal world, she would keep this coin forever. But two pounds was two pounds. There was *Mr Hatter* in the three-thirty for instance. Or lunch. She could take it back to the squat and eat in comfort. She'd have to pack her things anyway. Now that Simon had seen her she'd have to move on.

She wrapped her battered collecting tin in the blanket and

stuffed them into the rucksack. She liked this pitch. She was going to miss it. Hitching the bag over her shoulder, she crossed to the litter bin. Simon's card fluttered downwards, landing in a puddle of coffee at the bottom of a cardboard cup, coffee as dark as those eyes that she could still see awash with sympathy. She took a deep breath and straightened her shoulders. She would take the long way home; that way she would avoid the bookies.

Butterflies

by Meg Macleod

a white butterfly had fluttered at his graveside

now
here
in this time
there are butterflies everywhere
forever at the point of departure

reflected in the mirror
a picture hanging slightly off centre-
a painting of butterflies
echoed by wings of many colours
resting on the wooden frame

they are with me in the night
gentle irregular wingbeats
in my ribcage
moving me from sleeping
to waking to making tea
in the darkest early hours of winter

Legacy

by J. L Brook

I'd waited weeks for this moment. Hours of preparation, setting up the cameras and the dolly rig, trying different positions, different speeds. Then finally, it started happening…

I'd found her on a leaf in the garden. She was just an egg. A very shiny yellow egg stuck on the back of a red leaf. I'm a cameraman for the local TV station and they are always interested in local stories…this could be my big break…Look out David Attenborough, Danny Moreton is right behind you!

I carefully took the egg—not exactly sure what it was at this stage, but I set it carefully in a large glass tank that, years ago, held my long-gone tropical fish. I made the best environment possible for it and presumed it would be a butterfly.

I watched it develop and grow into a caterpillar; it was then that I could identify it. It was an Atlas Moth. A huge thing that I knew would become extremely beautiful...although I'm not entirely sure what an Atlas moth was doing in my garden, I'm always grateful for a story I can sell to TV producers.

The caterpillar grew, and as I learned which leaves it liked to munch on, it grew even bigger. Then one day, it could grow no more and started forming a chrysalis. Fascinating stuff, all the ridges, layers and dull grey and brown colours. I'd never seen this for real before. It was then that I began to set up my camera kit... I wanted to capture the moment when it emerged. I had plenty of set-up choices, my slow-mo and macro lenses would be perfect for the job. Then I waited, and waited...had it died in there, in its little shroud?

I set the camera to start filming at any hint of movement, so when I came downstairs on Wednesday morning and the process had already begun, I knew I hadn't missed anything. I was like a kid at Christmas.

All my preparations had come down to these next few hours. I stared in wonderment as it hatched, unfurled and dried out. It took over two hours and my cameras didn't fail. I got it from all angles, moving around the creature with the mini dolly rig. Just exquisite camera work; Mr Attenborough would be proud!

The last part was for it to pump its wings full of blood and expand them for the first time ever.

Errmm...wait, where's my book of moths? I flicked through it...A...for...Atlas...that is NOT an Atlas moth.

The wings grew bigger, longer and more solid. As they flapped, I could feel the wind from them. The tank, although huge, could not now contain its wingspan, so it climbed. It dragged its heavy black and purple body to the edge of the tank and hovered, its body kept aloft by silent, giant wings.

Did it just look at me? Were those tiny, shiny teeth? I was in the greenhouse. The windows were open and the doors were wide apart...what was I thinking?...then, as if IT knew what I was thinking, puff, it took flight.

Clumsy at first, it headed straight for the open door, its wings only JUST missing the frame. I was too shocked to think. I stood there, mouth open. I suddenly came to my senses and grabbed my smartphone. I took a few terrible shots of it as it flew into the daylight...daylight...definitely NOT a moth...what the heck was it? What has just been unleashed onto the world?

♦♦♦

The giant moth circled the trees in the garden and swooped onto a large dead branch. It stayed there, not moving... waiting... watching Danny. He was mesmerised, staring back, blinking occasionally. A tractor broke the spell as it drove past the end of the garden, hooting its horn as a hello. Danny could no longer stand by and gawk at this creature—he needed to research it.

His family had always had a thing for natural history and their old house was more like a museum than a family home. In every room and along every corridor were bookcases and stuffed creatures and, Danny realised, quite a lot of pinned butterfly collections. As if this was the first time he was seeing them, he investigated each exhibit. Moving from room to room, Danny had never really taken much interest in them before, but now he needed to collect information and learn as much as possible. He needed to be prepared to ask the right questions or give the correct answers should the situation warrant police or ambulances. Maybe one of the collections held a clue.

On the third floor was Danny's grandmother's old study. Until recently, the house held three generations; Danny's grandmother; Iris, Danny's mother; Lynda, and himself. Granny Iris had died only two years ago and the place was pretty much as she'd left it, albeit a bit dustier, as Lynda could not bear to disturb the room.

Danny approached the study. It was almost a sacred space. As a kid, he was banned from entering and as an adult, Iris had always been in the room observing him whenever he went in. The room was dark. Danny found a couple of old pull cords that turned on some dim lights. He saw more pinned moth collections under glass with ornate frames alongside plenty of old, hand-painted, illustrated books, which were mostly about butterflies and moths. Then it dawned on him that his granny's study was ONLY filled with butterflies and moths. Iris, it seemed, was a lepidopterist or at least had some sort of fascination with these delicate winged creatures.

After digging around his grandmother's collections of handwritten journals and newspaper clippings, Danny found a tiny book bound in a ribbon. It contained Iris's memoirs and a detailed description of the moth he had just let escape. It told about a childhood bedtime story and a little ditty song he'd forgotten about.

An image of his sister and his grandmother singing together immediately swept across his memory, taking him back to when he was little. The smell of the old oak furniture and beeswax polish, Granny's smile and soft skin was a comforting memory, spoiled only by Danny's inability to linger there. He looked out of the window. The creature was still waiting and, with a fresh sense of urgency. He continued reading Iris's diary.

♦ Iris's Story ♦

Iris's Diary — Monday 31st March 1930

For the third year, Father has entrusted me with clerical work at the mill. He shouts terribly, but again I have requested the small room on the spindle floor so as not to hear him. It is noisy and dusty, but I get to wave at my friend as she tends to the machines and best of all, I am not in Father's way.

Iris's diary—Friday 6th June 1930

Today I found a rather odd thing. I think it is an egg, although not like any egg I've ever encountered before. On my walk home from the mill, I spotted a large red leaf on the ground. It was pretty and unusual, so I collected it. Turning it over, I saw something round and shiny like a jellied marble stuck to the leaf. I've carefully brought it home and put it in a shoe box. I plan to study it, watch it hatch and see what comes out. Father has plenty of insect books, so I'll try to identify this egg.

Iris's diary — Monday 9th June 1930

It has hatched. It's a tiny caterpillar. I looked in Father's books but could not find this egg or caterpillar in any of them. I have no idea what to feed it. So I've collected leaves and flowers from all around the garden and so far, it's eating everything.

Iris's Diary—Tuesday 10th June 1930

I raced home from the mill today and accidentally left my umbrella in the cloakroom at work. I hope it doesn't rain tomorrow. It was worth it though, because the caterpillar has changed. Already it has doubled in size and, according to Father's books, that's not exactly normal. Its bright green body feels like a plump shrimp and has purple hairs running down its back. I haven't identified this creature. It could be new to science. I could be famous!

Iris's diary—Wednesday 11th June 1930

Today, when I finished typing, I sneaked over to Ellen at the spindle machine. She let me touch the thread and I helped her unclog stray fibres from a pin. But I cut myself across all my fingers like a paper cut. It hurt terribly. I thought better than to show Father as he would send me home and never let me return. So I stemmed the bleeding on the hem of my dress and got home as quickly as I could.

After I washed my dress with soap, I went to sit with the caterpillar. It tickled as it crawled over my hand, but that's not so strange as what happened to the cotton cuts on my fingers. I swear that this caterpillar licked the wounds, paying close attention to the deepest cuts. I didn't feel a thing, but after returning it to the box, I noticed that where the wounds had been open and leaking, now they were closed, knitted together with silk.

Iris's Diary — Thursday 12th June 1930

It's eating anything I put in front of it! Any leaf, flower or berry I bring it. It even ate a bit of ham that accidentally dropped in the box from my sandwich last night. My fingers—gosh—they feel like new. There's no pain, no scar; it's some kind of miracle or magic. Shame she has to grow up so fast, she'll soon fly away and I'll never have her help again. I daren't tell Father, he will say I am mad.

Iris's diary—Saturday 14th June 1930

The delicate lace cocoon it has spun around itself is the size of my hand, snowy white and feels exceptionally soft to stroke. by all accounts, this should turn into a hard case, brown and papery, then it will emerge, a new creature altogether.

Iris's diary—Monday 23rd June 1930

The mill is closed and Father is angry, but I knew something was special about today. I kept out of everyone's way and remained in my room with my caterpillar. This beautiful creature that healed my hands; I have cared for it, fed it and today, it hatched. A special day indeed.

Its appearance was not exactly what I expected, although I suppose nothing has been common about this creature. The cocoon cracked, peeled and a very large fluffy body emerged. Its wings were sorry looking, wet and drab. I think it's some kind of moth.

It climbed the twigs I had placed in the box and balanced on the edge. It was as still as a picture and then it began to grow. Its body filled and its wings expanded as fluid pumped through the veins. The delicate structures became thicker and longer. It was now twice as big as its box and my heart thumped in my throat. I swear that it looked at me as it took flight and perched on the rafters of my room.

I watched it. It made no noise, it just stared straight back at me. I have no idea what it wants now. Even when I opened the window, it remained steadfast.

Iris's diary — Tuesday 24th June 1930

As best I can manage, I've drawn the creature in the style of Father's illustrations. Trying to capture its size and beauty. Its markings and features. It really is wondrous. Yet it just stares at me.

Iris's Diary — Wednesday 25th June 1930

I woke this morning with a layer of dust all over my face; it stained my nightdress and pillow. I thought maybe there had been a storm overnight. Sometimes dust from the fields gets whipped up by the wind and covers Father's car. But I checked through my window and it seemed to only affect my room, my bed, and above me…was the moth. It had been shedding dust all over me. Was it dying? It certainly hadn't eaten anything for the past few days.

Iris's Diary - Thursday 26th June 1930

The air around me smells sweeter than before. My lungs fill so easily. My Father's physician had once told me that I had a lung disease, but today I feel like never before. Nothing has changed except not working at the mill and this creature emerging and shedding dust all over me. Now, I must admit that breathing in the cotton dust is sometimes painful, so not being at the mill must be a nice rest for my poor lungs. Still, I've had breaks before—Father took me to the south coast for medicinal purposes, but I didn't feel much better. Therefore my recovery must have something to do with the dust from the creature. So I swept up the dust and poured it into a glass jar. It was a miraculous caterpillar; maybe this is a miraculous moth, too?

Iris's Diary — Saturday 28th June 1930

Mother has had an accident. She burned her arm while cooking. The wound smelled awful and oozed. As she went upstairs for the ointment, I followed her, nipping into my room to get the jar of dust. Mother let me help her apply the cream. She was squeamish and looked away. I think she felt rather queasy. It was then I had my chance. I sprinkled some dust over Mother's arm, applied the ointment and set a bandage.

Mother is still in pain. She can't use her arm. I will prepare dinner and let her sleep.

Iris's Diary - Sunday 29th June 1930

Miraculous indeed! Mother's pain has vanished. I woke early to set the fire, but Mother was already up. Fire roaring and porridge cooking. She said that she felt much better and planned to check the wound.

I helped her again because she was nervous about the sight. As I unrolled the cloth from her arm, there was no smell, no ooze. I wiped away some debris and could not believe what I saw…perfect, beautiful skin. Mother was confused. She thought maybe she had dreamed it, blaming it on too much sleep tonic. But I assured her the injury yesterday was real…just as her recovery today was also real.

Taking a deep breath, I explained about the dust, the cuts on my fingers and my breathing. Mother believed me…although I didn't tell her about the creature, I told her it was pollen from a flower I had never seen before. It was wonderful to share this with her, albeit not the whole story. Mother made me promise to conserve this dust and collect more if I could, but to only use it for the most important of injuries. I did as she asked.

Iris's Diary — Sunday 13th July 1930

The mill re-opened a few days ago and I've been back at my typing machine (and waving at Ellen), but the week has been overwhelmingly hot and busy. Thankfully, Father did not need me yesterday, so I'd had an afternoon to myself. The week had been long with note-taking and following Father's new instructions. My fingers once again bled, this time, however, not from Ellen's thread, but from the stacks of papers I had to fold.

The sun was strong and the field behind the house was peaceful. I walked into the middle of the field where an old tree cast a shadow. Like a guardian angel, my giant moth followed me. She flew low, then swooped up to a branch and watched over me as I lay down in the warm grass. I felt safe and became sleepy in the summer breeze. I was fading into a dream when she swooped down and wrapped her giant leathery wings over and around me. I was cocooned, arms pushed against my chest, legs squeezed tightly together. There was a vibration. The creature shook and there was a cloud of dust in the air. I was powerless. I inhaled it. It fell on my eyes, my skin. It smelled sweet, like boiled liquorice. The dust made me delirious, made me relax and succumb to the beast.

There was no pain as the creature pierced my neck. It buried its long tongue into my sinews and I could feel it quivering and moving through my veins. It was lapping like a hummingbird on a flower. I paid no attention; I didn't mind the odd feeling, for I was drowsy and dreamed of lazy walks in the woods, of burrowing deep into the earth and feeling safe.

When I awoke, it was nighttime, nearly dawn. I was cold because the misty air had left a fine dew on my skin. I was standing under the tree next to a small hole with a shovel in my hand. The hole, despite only being two feet wide, was very deep. I was confused. I knew I had dug this hole but could not remember how or why.

The creature appeared. My moth, bigger than I'd ever seen her. She walked across the ground, dragging her wings against the soil and roots. She skulked heavily towards the hole and poured herself, head first, into the blackness. I dutifully refilled the earth and replaced the fallen leaves to hide what I had done. I knew I would never see her again.

    Stoically, I walked back to the house and up to my room. I undressed and fell into bed. It was over and the only thing I had left was my jar of healing dust.

♦♦♦

From Iris's descriptions in her diary and the beautiful illustrations, Danny instantly knew that this was the same moth creature that he had nurtured. The story was fantastical but seemed to match his experiences so far. He was fascinated and horrified at what might occur next. Danny recalled the song that Iris sang to him and his sister when they were children:

> *See an egg, care for it.*
> *Let it grow and do not quit.*
> *For it will hatch and fly nearby,*
> *Dance in the dust and never die.*
> *But there is always a price to pay.*
> *That day will come but do not pray.*
> *Leather wings will bind,*
> *And food it finds,*
> *Before it sleeps till daughter's time*

Danny's mother, Lynda, was returning home from an afternoon shopping. He heard the kitchen door bang in the breeze and leapt down the flights of stairs. He began asking her questions about Granny Iris and why she liked butterflies so much. This became a gentle introduction to the admittance that he'd been in Iris's study and, producing the diary bound in ribbon, he explained what he'd read. Tentatively, he asked Lynda what she knew about the bedtime story.

♦ Lynda's Story ♦

Lynda had a brief moment of shock and panic, but that soon gave way to acceptance. She had been waiting for this moment to come and perfecting her speech for years. She made them both a cup of hot cocoa and they sat in the drawing room. Like a rite of passage, Lynda began to tell Danny her story, the true events of her own encounters with the creature.

'Your granny, my mother, sang the same song to me as a child and I never understood it; it was just a sleepy bedtime rhyme. But when I was in my early twenties, much the same age as you are now, I found an egg. Something stirred in my memory and I knew I had to care for it.

The day came when it needed to eat more than leaves…I was scared, remembering Granny's tale. She had prepared me and told me all about what was to come, but of course, until it happened to me, I still hoped it was just a silly bedtime story.

Looking back, I think that knowing what was coming was worse than it being a complete surprise. I watched it make its chrysalis and hatch and grow each day with more dread knotting in my stomach. I collected the dust and the creature followed me, waiting for its moment.

When the actual act happened to me, it was late summer and I was gently napping in bed with the creature poised above me. With a thud, heavier than any dog, it dropped onto my mattress and wrapped its wings around me. Before I could call out, the dust had settled over my face and I fell into a drowsy, blissful state of hypnotic dream. Then, it was over so quickly. I remember it diving into the hole that I'd dug under an apple tree. I remember the blisters I had on my hands for days afterwards, but I could not recall anything between the bed and the orchard.

I'd collected the dust, just like Granny had before me and, true to the story, it had healing powers, your dad and I have lived a very healthy life. Then we had you and your sister and I knew I had to prepare Alice, too.'

Lynda faltered, her memories becoming painful. When twins, Danny and Alice were born, Lynda knew that she must tell them the same bedtime stories. She wanted them to be prepared for their encounter...of course, she explained it more clearly to Alice. Being female seemed to be part of this creature's legacy.

But, at the age of twelve, Danny and his sister were in an accident and despite being given every last remaining drop of the dust that her mum had kept, Alice did not survive. So, Danny has now been chosen. It was time to fulfil his destiny.

Even though Danny had not recalled the prophetic bedtime story, he had still instinctively followed in his family's footsteps. Of course, now, he knew what came next and was afraid, but his mother and grandmother had both gone through the ordeal and survived. So he would do it too, claim his reward and, one day, pass on the legacy to his own daughter.

Blitz

by Margaret Mackay

A true story

It was early Spring. Our country was at war. The full moon rose high above the horizon. *'A bomber's moon'* is what the men who stood on the corner of the street called it. Its shimmering glow was the only light in the row of burnished brick, terraced houses, one of which, was home to me and my family.

My baby sister was one year and five months old on the night of the thirteenth of March, 1941. That was the night the Luftwaffe launched the most devastating air raid on my home town of Clydebank, largely destroying it; of 12,000 houses, only seven remained undamaged. It was also the scene of the worst civilian loss of life in all of Scotland. Hundreds of people were injured. Five hundred and twenty-eight souls perished in the Blitz; I'm happy to say I was one of the survivors.

It was a fairly typical Thursday night in No 12 Livingstone Street. My father and eldest brother were already serving soldiers. The two eldest girls had left for their night shift at the munitions factory, the two younger boys were at the pictures and my mother was two streets away having her hair done. It had fallen to me, the fourteen-year-old big sister to look after the baby. My mother had bathed her and tucked her up in her cot before she left.

'Shouldn't be too long, half eight at the latest, Cissie's staying late to do my perm, Don't forget your homework,' said my mother as she hurried through the door.

I munched the last of my sweetie ration as I got to grips with an essay on Wuthering Heights. The music of Carrol Gibbon's orchestra came to an end with the announcement of the Nine O'clock News. I'll give that a miss, I thought; it was all about the war these days.

As I uncurled myself from the cosy depths of the fireside chair, the sound of a siren that began with a low whine turned into a deafening wail that filled the space around me.

Over the last few months, there had been many false alarms. Did I dare look through a chink in the blackout? I could just imagine old Sandy the air-raid warden shouting at me, 'Put that bloody light out.' I was about to do that when an ear-splitting blast caused the walls of the house to shudder. The lights went out. This was no false alarm! I groped my way to the stairs. My baby sister was up there. With each step I took, the house groaned and squeaked like a creaking cart. The only sound coming from the cot was the steady breathing of the sleeping child.

I wrapped her blankets around her, took the pillow from under her head and gently lifted her into my arms. A chubby fist shot out of my precious bundle as another resounding blast echoed through the house. The smell of baby soap, the soft silkiness of her curls against my cheek as I carried her downstairs, was balm to my fear. With each step, the handrail of the bannister shook beneath my already trembling hand.

I'd take her to the safest place I know, a play fortress of brick where my brothers and I had held out against imaginary savage hordes of marauding pirates, Apaches and packs of hungry wolves. The tower where the princess waited to be rescued by her knight in shining armour. As I crossed the backcourt flames rose high in the sky, and the outline of Singer's clock tower glowed like a burning beacon. As I turned the key in the lock of the wash house another earth-shattering explosion came at me from out of the night.

Once inside, my knees shook as I stepped up onto the slatted duckboard and removed the wooden lid of the boiler. As I placed my little sister into the depths of the concrete vault, she whimpered. I put her dummy in her mouth and she settled down. I sat down on a stool. As I pulled the quilt around my shoulders, a dreaded thought came to me. My mother will kill me for taking her satin quilt into the wash house.

I'd taken my book with me but the only light that filtered through the mottled window came from the moon. Would reading about Heathcliffe and Cathy's love have stopped my hands from shaking? I was a member of the school choir but fear sat like a knot in my throat when I tried to sing.

Up until that moment, I'd only been concerned about the baby. Tears welled up as I thought of the other members of my family. Everyone said the Germans were desperate to destroy the Clydeside shipyards and munitions factories. My big sisters worked in Singer's. I had uncles and cousins in John Brown's. Would the boys be okay in the cinema? My poor mother will be going frantic.

And so it went on, strike after strike, a helter-skelter of flying debris, The urgent screams of ambulances and fire engines and sounds I'd never heard before. And still, my baby sister slept.

At some stage during the night, as I sat there, hands over my ears trying to blank out the noise, sleep overtook my terror. I was awakened by hurrying footsteps and my brother, Jack's voice. 'I bet I know where they are.'

The door flew open and I ran to my mother's arms. A whimper followed by a lusty cry of outrage filled the tiny space; the baby had decided to contribute to the general mayhem.

'She's put Margaret in the boiler,' said my younger brother, James. Mother was at first a little concerned that the baby should be placed in such an unusual hiding place but quickly realised that it was probably the safest option given the danger caused by collapsing structures and falling masonry potentially trapping Clydesiders under tons of immovable debris.

The following night when the siren sounded, armed with a bulging bag of practical possessions and her four youngest children, my mother queued up at the entrance to the air raid shelter to spend the night in relative safety, away from the dangers so apparent the previous evening The following morning as she and her neighbours emerged into the watery sunshine, the terrace that had been their homes was a fire-scarred crumbling ruin. The wash houses that had sat in the back courts had disappeared, along with thousands of houses, hundreds of Clydesiders, John Brown's shipyards and a large section of the Singer factory. Everyone emerging from the air raid shelters that morning realised how lucky they had been; they may not have had a home or any possessions but they were alive and grateful for that.

My sister and I had avoided annihilation by a mere twenty-four hours.

Altnabreac

by John Knowles

Screeching brakes, a loud hiss and the two-carriage train came to a shuddering halt. Looking out of the window, Iona spotted a tall, slim woman standing on the platform beside a dilapidated wooden shelter. Her long black coat and cape cocooned her from the cold December air, its hood obscuring her features. Iona had travelled this line many times, but not once had the train stopped at the lonely request stop of Altnabreac. She was intrigued. The hamlet was literally in the middle of nowhere, its three cottages served only by a bumpy forest track and the railway. Outside a swirling mist clung to the heather-clad moor, like a gossamer duvet. The driver hopped out briefly, picking up a parcel from the wooden shelter, before returning to the train. He didn't seem to notice the woman standing on the platform. It was only four in the afternoon and already getting dark. With squeaking tired hinges, the door to Iona's carriage opened. A blast of icy air swept through the carriage followed by the woman. Pulling down her hood, Iona saw that the woman was young, about the same age as herself. She had a thin face, with a pallid complexion and long dark bedraggled hair. She looked sad as if she hadn't a friend in the world.

'Hello, it's a bit of a chilly one today isn't it' Iona said cheerfully. The woman didn't reply but simply nodded. She sat down at the other end of the carriage, resting her hands in her lap. Why didn't she speak, Iona thought. Maybe she had a lot on her mind or maybe she was just shy. Oh well, she'd been civil to the woman, which was all she could do. Iona was tired after a busy day, catching up with friends in Inverness. Her home in Thurso was only a few miles away now. The thought of a hot meal and a log fire was enticing.

With a sudden jolt, the train moved off toward Thurso. Picking up speed the rhythmic clickety-clack of the wheels was having a hypnotic effect on her. Iona's eyes were feeling heavy now, her breathing deeper. Her eyelids soon closed out her surroundings, as the rhythm of the train took her away to a land far beyond Caithness.

All of a sudden, Iona woke with a start. To her surprise, she was on the floor. The train was stationary now and her carriage was in total darkness. She shivered. It felt as if a strange freezing mist had woven itself around her body. Panicking, she clawed for her seat and tried to haul herself upright. Suddenly she felt someone or something touch her hair. She screamed, spinning around in panic, looking into the blackness around her. All of a sudden light once again flooded the carriage. The carriage door promptly opened and a man she assumed was the driver appeared. 'Are you alright lass?' The driver was of medium build, around fifty years of age with short greying hair. His face was reddened and his brow furrowed with worry. 'You pulled the emergency cord lass. Is there a problem?'

'It wasn't me,' Iona replied indignantly. The man seemed surprised at her denial. 'It must have been you. We're the only people on the train, and it certainly wasn't me.' With a heavy sigh, Iona tried to hide her frustration. 'I'm telling you; I didn't pull the emergency cord. Maybe the woman who boarded at Altnabreac pulled it.'

'Woman, what woman,' the driver said seemingly puzzled. 'As I said, we're the only ones on board.'

'It must have been the Altnabreac woman,' Iona retorted angrily.

Losing patience, the driver replied, 'Look, I told you, nobody boarded at Altnabreac. Granted, I did pick up a parcel, but no passengers.'

Iona's face glowed red as rage surged through her body. 'I saw her get on with my own eyes. She sat over there.' Iona stabbed a finger towards an empty seat in the corner.

'So where is she now? She can't have just disappeared into thin air.'

'Oh, I don't know! Maybe she got off.'

The driver chuckled. 'Got off! No one in their right mind would try and get off a moving train, let alone in the middle of nowhere.'

Iona knew she couldn't argue with that, but was adamant she'd seen the woman. As she pushed her long red hair from her face, the driver could see tears of frustration welling up in Iona's deep blue eyes. Her mascara started to run and she was shaking.

The driver gave her a sympathetic smile. 'I'm sorry if I upset you lass, but we do have to investigate if the emergency cord is activated. I think the best thing would be to get on our way and say no more about it.' With that, he went back to his cab and they continued on their way.

They'd only been moving for a couple of minutes when suddenly the carriage lights started to flicker and the train lost power. Iona sighed. *Oh my God, what's up now*, she thought.

The train ground to a halt. Looking out of the window, she saw nothing but the fading light from the western sky. A flake of snow stuck to her window, followed almost immediately by another. Quietness enveloped her as she sat there under the now-dimmed lights.

After a short while, the door to her carriage opened and the driver appeared once again, sweat on his brow, oil on his hands. 'Something's wrong with the loco, I'm afraid lass. I've tried to fix it but the problem is way beyond my capabilities. It'll need a proper mechanic to repair the old girl I'm afraid. I've no way of reporting the problem from the cab.

Iona fished a mobile phone out of her handbag. The words, '*low battery*' flickered momentarily on the screen before it went black. 'I was going to say, use this, but the bloody battery appears to be dead.' He stared at the phone open-mouthed.

'What the matter? Haven't you seen a mobile phone before?'

'Of course I have,' he said indignantly, trying to hide his obvious embarrassment. 'I just don't have one myself.' However, his initial expression said it all as far as Iona was concerned.

'So what are we going to do,' Iona enquired impatiently.

Stroking the stubble on his chin, the driver thought for a moment. 'I'm going to have to walk back to Altnabreac and telephone for help from there. You stay here and I'll be back in about two hours.'

The blood drained from Iona's face as if she'd seen a ghost. 'Two hours! I'm not staying out here all alone for two hours.'

The driver sighed. 'You'll be okay here; there are no more trains due along this line today. I'll be as quick as I can.'

Iona saw her reflection in the window, realising to her horror how drawn and haggard she looked despite being just twenty-three years of age.

'No! I'm not staying here all on my own. The carriage lights aren't going to last much longer by the look of them, so if you think I'm going to sit here in the middle of nowhere in total darkness, you're very much mistaken.'

Somehow he knew he wasn't going to win this argument. 'Okay, I suppose you could come with me, but it's quite a walk back.'

Iona smiled. 'Nay problem. They build us lassies tough up here in Caithness."

Following the tracks, they made their way back by the light of the driver's torch. Iona's shoes slipped on the icy sleepers. She wished she'd chosen to travel in her walking boots instead of shoes. Stumbling on, she was soon finding the weight of her backpack, a burden she could well have done without.

Looking back, the driver saw that Iona was losing ground on him. He stopped to let her catch up. 'Shall I carry your backpack for a while lass?'

She smiled. 'Thanks, that would be great Mr engine driver.'

Chuckling, he took the pack from her and slung it over his

shoulder. 'The name's Stuart, Stuart Sutherland, and you?'

'Iona Gunn,' she replied.

They trudged on for what seemed like an eternity. Large white flakes were now coming down at an alarming rate, driven against her body by the increasingly strong wind. The strength of the icy blasts cut through her clothing; the wind felt as if it would blow her over.

'Are you sure this is a good idea?' she called out. Her words swept away on the howling wind. The rails and sleepers were rapidly disappearing under a blanket of powdery snow. Trudging on, her leg muscles burned with fatigue and tears welled up in her eyes.

'Stuart, for pity sake, stop, I can't keep up.' Her scream was more a demand than a request.

Stuart turned round to see her just standing there.

'Stuart, I can't go on. We should have stayed with the train.'

Stuart raised an eyebrow. 'I thought you said Caithness lassies were built tough.'

Her look of indignation conveyed the reaction he'd expected.

'We are tough, but trying to walk along an icy railway line in these shoes would be enough to defeat Sir Edmund Hillary.'

He gave her a wan smile. 'Come on lass, we can't stop now. by my reckoning, we'll be back at Altnabreac in half an hour.'

'Well I hope you're right,' Iona replied, knowing in reality she had no choice but to trust him. She stumbled on through the snow, her feet losing traction.

True to his word, half an hour later the hazy form of the station building loomed through the still-heavy snowfall. A sense of relief surged through her body as she staggered up to the platform.

Stuart found the key hidden under a large plant pot. He gave the door a hefty shove with his shoulder and fell into the room. Switching on the light revealed a large, spartan room where a musty odour permeated the place and it felt damp.

Iona surmised that the old building would rarely have been occupied. The floor had been constructed from local Caithness flagstone. On the far wall was an open fire, a pile of logs beside it. Two armchairs had been placed on either side of the fireplace. In the opposite corner was a shabby desk with an equally ragged leather chair. A telephone that looked like a prop from a Laurel and Hardy movie sat upon the battered wooden desktop.

Iona walked across to the desk and examined the old phone. 'Good grief, this is rather old, isn't it? I'd have thought Scot Rail would have ditched these phones years ago, even out here.'

'Why would they do that, when this one works perfectly fine?' Stuart said scornfully.

Iona shrugged, too tired to pursue the matter.

Picking up the receiver he dialled the number for Thurso railway station. Iona watched as the dial whirred round with each number.

'Weird but pretty cool never the less,' she said, smiling.

'Um, what isn't quite so cool, as you put it, is that the line's dead. The storm must have brought the wires down.'

Iona pulled her mobile out of her pocket. The screen surprisingly showed she had a little charge left, but to her frustration, the words *No Signal* shone out dimly from the screen. She turned to him. 'I'm afraid I can't get a signal. '

Stuart frowned. 'What do you mean?'

'No signal means no phone call,' Iona retorted.

He sighed. 'It looks like we're going to be stranded for some time. We'll have to hunker down here for the night. With our train not arriving at Thurso, the emergency services will have been alerted. It could take hours for them to get out here, especially in these conditions. I suggest we get the fire lit and try and get some rest.'

It wasn't long before the warm glow of the fire was thawing them out. It was then that she saw it. She hadn't noticed the portrait above the fireplace until now. Iona pointed up at the faded photograph surrounded by a simple wooden frame. Her hand trembled.

'It's her.'

Her sudden outburst made Stuart jump. 'For goodness sake, what on earth is the matter?'

'It's the woman on the train,' Iona replied, still pointing at the photograph.

Stuart sighed. 'I told you; there was no other woman on the train.'

A sudden rush of red coloured her cheeks as she felt the hackles rise.

'I know what I saw,' she said with stubborn defiance.

All of a sudden there was a loud crackle as the logs in the grate shifted, sending a volley of sparks darting up the chimney like shooting stars.

'It can't be the same person. This photograph looks very old.'

Moving closer, Iona could see a name written in neat script on the picture mount. 'Lizzy Coghill. I wonder who Lizzy Coghill was?'

Stuart looked blankly back at her. 'I've heard the name mentioned, but know nothing about her.'

'I'm positive it's her,' Iona said. 'It's those sad eyes, they're so distinctive.'

The look of irritation on Stuart's face was unmistakable. 'Oh don't start that one again lass. I told you, there were only two of us on the train, nobody else.'

They sat in front of the fire for a couple of hours, chattering as if they'd known each other for years. The subject of Lizzy Coghill was dropped, but Iona decided that once she got home she'd do some research.

When the last of the fire's flames had died leaving just the red glow of the embers, Stuart had already dozed off, so she decided that maybe she should try and get some sleep too. It wasn't long before she fell into a deep slumber.

Iona became aware of an ethereal mist swirling around her ankles. She seemed to be on a sheep track that cut across the heather-covered moor. She felt weightless, drifting silently across the frozen ground. A faint glimmer in the western sky was the only thing to light her way. Not once did she ask herself why she was out on the moor at this late hour. It seemed perfectly logical as if she'd been drawn outside by some unseen power. Then, in the distance, she saw the faint figure of a young woman coming toward her. As the woman moved closer, Iona could see that she was very young.

Her heart leapt into her mouth, realising that she recognised her. It was Lizzy Coghill. She wore a dark blue dress with a white shawl around her shoulders.

'Hello, Lizzy,' Iona said. Iona received no reply, indeed no recognition that she was there at all. The woman looked straight ahead, a distressed expression on her chalk-white face.

The sudden loud crash of breaking glass broke into her dream, causing her to leap up from her chair. Jagged shards were strewn across the stone floor. The frame of the picture lay splintered, the photograph covered with pieces of shattered glass. She momentarily panicked as the shock stole her breath away. It was then that she noticed Stuart wasn't there. Almost in disbelief, Iona scanned the room. Opening the door she frantically glanced left and then right.

'Stuart, where are you?' she bellowed. There was no reply. Her heart thumped against her rib cage, and beads of sweat dotted her brow despite the cold weather.

'If this is some sort of a joke, it's not funny.' The silence was deafening. The only sound was the plaintive cry of a bird of prey wheeling above her. *Perhaps he's gone back to the train*, she thought, although why he would do so she'd no idea.

Trudging through the snow for what seemed like hours, she finally saw the abandoned train in the distance. There was no visible sign of life as she approached.

'Stuart, are you there?' Her heart sank when no reply was forthcoming. It was a long way up into the carriage, but somehow she managed to haul herself in. The carriage was empty, and snow had built up on the windows, making it difficult to see out. Passing through to the second carriage proved fruitless. Accessing the locomotive's cab would be difficult, but she knew she had to check it out. Heaving herself up the cab steps, she found the door locked. She quickly wiped the snow away from the window and peered in. Her scream was lost in the vastness of the moor. She almost fell back into the snow at the sight that met her eyes. Inside, sitting bolt upright, was a tall man, his face as white as the snow. *Who was he and how had he ended up sitting in the locomotive?* All she did know, was it certainly wasn't Stuart.

Tumbling down from the cab steps, she fell into the snow, picked herself up and ran as fast as she could, despite the slippery conditions. She felt sick and confused but had to get away from the train. The sound of her pumping heart echoed in her ears and she was gasping for breath. Eventually, overcome by exhaustion, she collapsed. Glancing frantically back toward the train, she almost expected to see someone in pursuit, but there was no one there.

With tears flowing down her cheeks, she trudged back toward Altnabreac. When she eventually reached the station, she saw two men standing beside a Land Rover having a heated discussion. Iona stumbled towards them and fell with exhaustion.

The two men ran towards her and hauled her to her feet. Both wore thick day-glow jackets sporting the Scot Rail insignia.

'Are you okay, my dear?' the taller of the men enquired, a concerned frown on his face. Scott Mackay was about thirty, thick-set, with black curly hair protruding from beneath a Scot Rail Beeny hat.

'No, not really,' Iona whimpered.

'What on earth are you doing out here in this horrendous weather?' the shorter man interjected. Cameron O'Brien's bright red hair and beard stood out against the whiteness all around.

'Well I'm not out for an early morning stroll if that's what you're thinking,' she replied sarcastically. 'I was a passenger on the train that broke down yesterday. I trust you gentlemen have been sent to deal with the situation.'

'Aye, that's right. Where exactly did the train break down and where on earth is the driver?'

'The train's about an hour's walk, she replied.' Pointing up the line in the direction she had come. 'Stuart Sutherland, the driver and I walked back here to shelter for the night. In the morning he was gone. Why would he go off like that?'

'Presumably to get help,' Cameron said.

Iona sighed. 'The crazy thing is, there's a man in the driver's cab but he doesn't look anything like Stuart Sutherland.' Her body shook violently as she thought about the horrific image she'd encountered. 'I think he's dead.'

'Now let's not get ahead of ourselves here,' Scott interjected. 'We can't be sure of that.'

'Well his face was as white as chalk and he didn't react when I knocked on the window.'

The air ambulance arrived within thirty minutes of Cameron's emergency call and flew the body of the driver through to Raigmore Hospital in Inverness. Iona's suspicions had been correct after all; Sandy McLeod had died at the scene from a heart attack. The thing that puzzled the paramedics was the look of sheer terror on his face.

The ensuing enquiry into Sandy McLeod's death was a traumatic experience for Iona who naturally was called upon to give evidence. The coroner, Douglas Henderson, listened intently as Iona gave her account of what had happened. Her insistence that the driver she'd met had been named Stuart Sutherland seemed to call into question her reliability as a witness.

'What about fellow passengers? Were there any other passengers on board at the time?' the coroner asked.

There was a slight pause before she was able to reply. 'No sir, I mean yes,' she stammered.

'You seem a little unsure about that, Miss Gunn.'

Iona's face suddenly reddened. She felt as if the walls of the room were closing in on her. She wanted to tell the truth but knew they'd think her a crank if she told them about the mysterious woman.

'Eh, sorry sir, I mean yes, I saw another woman get on at Altnabreac.'

'What did this alleged woman look like and what did she do once the train had come to a halt?'

Iona felt as if she would explode with anger. 'Alleged! What do you mean by alleged? That I'm making this all up?'

Douglas Henderson looked taken aback by her outburst. 'I'm sorry Miss Gunn, but I'm just trying to ascertain whether anyone else may have seen anything unusual that could have caused the driver to have a heart attack.'

46

Composing herself, Iona replied. 'She was tall, slim, about my age and was wearing a long black coat with a cape. Her face was pallid and drawn. She looked so sad.'

Coroner Henderson stroked his chin. 'So where did this woman go after the train broke down?'

Iona cleared her throat, her voice nervously wavering as she replied. 'When the lights came back on, she'd gone.'

'So you never saw her again?'

'No sir.'

When the coroner's report was concluded, Sandy McLeod's death was recorded as by natural causes.

Although with time, Iona's life returned to some semblance of normality, she always felt that there were still questions to be answered. Who was Stuart Sutherland and who was the mysterious woman she'd seen on the train? She simply had to find out the truth. She knew Stuart Sutherland was a common name in the north of Scotland, but only a tiny fraction would have worked on the railways.

Her first thought was to visit the Caithness Archive, housed at the Nucleus and Caithness Archive Centre in Wick. Maybe she could find out more about Lizzy Coghill's life and her unfortunate demise.

Black clouds hung menacingly over the triangular-shaped Nucleus building as Iona pulled into the car park. She hurried toward the entrance, as the first drops of an imminent downpour landed on her head. Sitting behind a large desk was a young woman tapping on a keyboard.

She looked up and smiled as Iona entered. 'Hello, how can I help?'

'Hi, I'm Iona Gunn. I'm looking for information regarding a railway accident at Altnabreac,' she replied with a smile.

'Oh yes, you telephoned to book an appointment. If you'd like to come this way, I'll get one of my colleagues to show you where to look.'

Iona was led down a long corridor lined with modern brightly lit offices. The corridor opened out into a large room filled with desks and cabinets. Each desk had a computer.

'It's your lucky day. We can just about squeeze you in,' the young woman said, chuckling as they surveyed the vastness of the empty room. 'Now if you need any help just let one of the staff know, and we'll do what we can to assist you.'

'Thank you, you've been most helpful,' Iona replied gratefully.

Iona looked blankly at the computer screen. Where should she start? She had no idea when this woman had lived or what had actually happened to her. She typed in the name Lizzy Coghill and pressed the enter key. A number of websites populated the screen. The one that caught her eye was a Caithness history site. Clicking on the link, a page full of photographs and script filled the screen. An old photograph confirmed she had the correct Lizzy Coghill, another depicted a lonely grave, way out on the moors. She started reading.

Elizabeth (Lizzy) Coghill was born in the remote hamlet of Altnabreac in 1898. She was the only child of Hamish and Mary Coghill. At the tender age of sixteen, Lizzy became pregnant by a local lad, who panicked and ran off to join the army. Sex before marriage was frowned upon in those days, but to end up pregnant was even worse. Consequently, the local community, small though it was, ostracised her. The baby, a girl named Emily, was born soon after Lizzy's seventeenth birthday. The story goes that Lizzy's life was made so miserable, that in 1918, she threw herself in front of a train. Lizzy Coghill was buried in unhallowed ground way out on the moor at Altnabreac. Emily was initially taken care of by her Grandparents, but when both tragically died of fever, a couple in Thurso adopted the young child. Legend has it that Lizzy's ghost still wanders the lonely moor, looking for her lost child.'

A single tear fell onto Iona's notebook, smudging some of her notes. How could people be so cruel to drive this young woman to suicide? Now Iona was even more convinced that it was Lizzy she'd seen on the train and in her strange dream. What Iona couldn't understand was why Lizzy had appeared to her and how

Stuart Sutherland fitted into the story. Was he real, or was he also a ghost? Determined to get to the bottom of the mystery, she set out to find out about the mysterious Stuart Sutherland. She'd asked at Thurso and Wick railway stations, but nobody had heard of him. Then a thought came into her mind. It was a long shot and would more than likely come to nothing. Maybe, just maybe, Stuart was the driver of the train that killed poor Lizzy all those years ago. Feeling guilty and grief-stricken, perhaps his restless soul was destined to roam the lonely moors forever. Iona could hardly believe she was thinking like this.

Surfing the Internet, Iona soon found a website where she could search for death records. Tapping in the name Sutherland, her screen was soon populated with thousands of entries. She'd have to be more specific. If Stuart were indeed a ghost, she'd try a search around the time of Lizzy's death. Although there were plenty of Sutherland deaths recorded for Caithness, not a single Stuart was listed. Maybe he'd been a relatively young man at the time of Lizzy's death. Her head in her hands, she shut her eyes and tried to focus her mind on the facts. She knew that Lizzy had died in 1918, so if the driver was, say, thirty at the time and he'd lived until he was seventy, he would have died around 1958. She typed in the relevant time period and Bingo, there he was. Stuart Sutherland died at the grand old age of seventy-seven in 1965 and was buried in Thurso cemetery.

As Iona stepped out of her silver two-seater Mercedes, a blast of icy wind almost took her door off its hinges. Pulling her up collar, she made her way into Thurso cemetery. She would have to be methodical, examining each row of gravestones in turn. Numerous flights of steps led down to the bottom of the cemetery. After fifteen minutes of searching, she'd found nothing. Her long sigh was lost in the wind.

She wondered whether she was in the wrong cemetery. As far as she was aware, there wasn't another cemetery in Thurso. Having descended to the Iron Gate that led out towards the river, she had resigned herself to failure. There was one more row of stones to examine. Halleluiah! At last there it was.

Here lies Stuart James Sutherland, born 8th January 1888, died 18th August 1965.

Underneath that inscription was another.

And wife Catherine Mary Sutherland, born 14th December 1893, died 7th May 1983 aged 90 years.

The inscription that followed shook Iona to the core. She could hardly believe what she was reading.

Also daughter, Emily Coghill – Sutherland, born 5th March 1917, died 17th April 2001 at the age of 84.

As she turned to leave, she caught sight of a figure standing by the river. It appeared to be a young woman holding a baby in her arms. The woman gave her a wan smile and within a fraction of a second, disappeared.

A walk at Twilight

by Sharon Gunason Pottinger

The dark comes in quickly
now it is November
the skyline rose pink
where the sun slips beneath the horizon
the moon rising low biscuit yellow
sliced neatly in half
the last load of hay on the back
of a hurrying tractor loud as thunder
passes through the stillness of twilight

dark time on this path to the swan's loch
is a different chapter in the book
where I insert myself
the pattern of my boots on the tarmac
among the hedgerow creatures
and the flowers of the verge
bird's foot trefoil vetch and gorse
yarrow looming in the light
of the moon and the evening star
a lonely planet cast adrift

the first cool of the evening
dances through my hair
I listen to the hard-working burn
cattle in the field shuffling breathing
a dog in the distance barking
my own heartbeat among these rhythms

the loch appears flat in the low light
swans sleeping huddled into themselves
pale shapes like waves frozen
into an artist's landscape
I breathe their stillness into me
and turn toward home beneath the light
of the half-moon and the lonely planet

The Witch on the Cliff

by Catherine Byrne

'Don't you dawdle on the way, doll,' shouted Flora as she saw her daughter off down the road. 'I'm longing for that cup o' tea.'

'I'll no be long, Mam,' answered Jemmy, but did not make any effort to speed up.

She trailed up the road to the mill with her tin container. Anabel McCallan had three cows and was always pleased to sell Flora milk when her cow was low on production, and, with a young calf to feed as well, this was at least twice a week.

'Ah, Jemmy, ma wee pet,' shouted Anabel. She was almost deaf and shouted most of the time. Jemmy's granda' had said her voice would double as a fog horn if ever there was a breakdown.

Although on the verge of tears, as she always was these days, Jemmy smiled. 'Mam needs a droppy of milk.' She held up the tin.

'Come away in, love.' Anabel led the way into the scullery and lifted the lid off the pail, which sat there. She dipped a ladle into the milk and filled Jemmy's container. 'And tell yer mam there'll be no charge. Now, have a cupful yersel, it's still warm. I've cooked treacle bannocks as well.' She filled a cup and led

Jemmy into the big, square kitchen.

Jemmy didn't like milk straight from the cow; she imagined it still bore the taste of the animal, but she was too polite to say so. Treacle bannocks were nice, but Jemmy hoped Anabel wouldn't spread them thick with home-churned butter or, worse still, crowdie.

'Would ye like some of my rhubarb jam?' Anabel asked as she cut the bannock.

Jemmy nodded. 'Yes, please.'

The door opened and Anabel's man, Bill, and son, Ten-year-old Malcolm came in.

'Ah, wee Jemmy,' said Bill and ruffled her hair. 'Are ye all right, pet?'

'I'm... I'm sorry about yer da,' stammered Malcolm avoiding her eye. His face grew pink. Jemmy glowered at him. He had once been her best friend, but he seemed to have been avoiding her since the death of her father.

Tears broke free from the battleground behind her eyes and trickled down her face and her bannock became difficult to swallow. Her da had been gone for over six months and the pain was still raw. Embarrassed, she wiped at her cheeks. Bill bent down and scooped her up in his arms. He smelled of the sea and peat smoke and pipe tobacco and his chin was rough against her skin, just like her da's had been. She put her arms around his neck and sobbed into the rough wool of his gansey.

When the storm of tears had passed, she still clung to him. In his arms, she felt warm and safe.

Anabel rubbed her back. 'Awe, lassie, calm yerself.' She eased the child from Bill's arms and pressed her to her massive bosom.

Eventually, in control, Jemmy allowed herself to be lowered into the kitchen chair, allowed Anabel to wipe the tears from her eyes, and reluctantly drank some of the warm, creamy milk that tasted of cow.

'Thanks. I have to go.' She grabbed what was left of her bannock and the container of milk and made for the door.

'Carry the milk for her, Malcolm,' ordered Bill.

Keeping his eyes lowered, he took the container from her.

She followed Malcolm up the road. 'Ye never came to see me,' she said to his silent back.

He shrugged his shoulders. 'I wanted to. I didn't know what to say, like.'

'That wasn't being a very good friend.'

'I'm sorry. I'm pleased I saw ye the day, though.'

Only a couple of years older than Jemmy, Malcolm was a stout lad, big for his age and almost as strong as a man. He wasn't afraid of anything and Jemmy admired him immensely.

At the bend in the road, she slowed down. To one side the land fell away to a narrow cove. From here they were high up and had a clear view of the sheer cliff and the jagged rocks at the other side of the bay. Today there were two people at the top of the opposite cliff and they seemed to be arguing.

'There's a man with the witch,' whispered Jemmy.

Reeva Donn was a strange, silent woman, whom no one knew much about or where she had come from. She'd recently moved into an abandoned cottage high on the outcrop and lived as a recluse, rebuffing any attempt at friendship. Exceptionally tall for a woman, but bent almost double and always dressed in black, with long, greying hair that hung across her face, she made a strange figure. Her only companions were a number of stray cats that had found their way to her door. The local children called her a witch and made up tales that grew more fanciful with every telling.

Jemmy, like most of the others, was afraid of her. She was narrow-mouthed with small dead eyes like a rat and a body that was all bone and angles. And she never spoke to anyone except to shout at the children when they dared each other to steal raspberries from her garden. If it wasn't for Malcolm and his mischief, Jemmy would have never ventured near the witch's abode at all. It was Malcolm who'd found out the witch's name, but he had never found out where she'd come from or why she was here.

As they watched, the couple came together and began to twist and turn in a macabre dance that took them nearer and nearer to the edge of the cliff. Suddenly the pair parted, the man staggered backwards and fell.

Malcolm grabbed Jemmy's arm and dragged her down behind a gorse bush. 'Don't let them see us,' he hissed. 'She's murdering someone.'

'How d'ye know?' asked Jemmy, 'he only fell,' but she allowed herself to be pulled down behind the bush anyway.

'I'm telling ye, she is.' Malcolm was always one for the drama, and for a moment, Jemmy saw this as another game. Of course, the man couldn't be dead, but it was fun to pretend.

Reeva stood still for a moment, then began to roll the man who offered no resistance, towards the edge of the cliff then pushed him over with her foot.

The children watched, transfixed in horror, as the reality hit them. The shape fell and unravelled, the arms and legs outstretched. And it bounced from rock to rock, down the cliff face until it disappeared into the swirling foam below. Reeva moved towards the cliff-top and peered over the edge.

'She...she killed a man,' said Jemmy in a whisper. 'Who...who is he?'

'I don't know. We'd better say nothing. She might come after us. Anyway, maybe he can swim, he might be all right.'

Jemmy's stomach clenched and she needed to pee. She had to get away before she disgraced herself in front of Malcolm. She tried to rise.

'Wait. Don't let her see ye.' Malcolm held her arm pinning her to the ground. They watched until Reeva turned around and headed back towards her cottage. She was limping and held her head low. One hand was pressed to her chest.

'Take the milk.' Malcolm thrust the container into Jemmy's hands. 'I'll get my dad.' And he ran and left her.

'My goodness, what's wrong? Ye look like ye've been chased by the de'il himself.' Flora took the can of milk from her daughter's shaking hands.

'Reeva Donn killed a mannie. She pushed him off the cliff.'

'Awe, come on now. Ye must be wrong. Where was this?'

'Just…just over the hill there.' Jemmy pointed through the window.

'I bet Malcolm was with ye. He's full o' these stories, and ye believe him,' said her grandfather, who was knitting a twine net attached to a hook on the wall. He pushed the large wooden needle through the last link, formed a knot and stretched it with his fingers until it was tight.

'It's true, it's no a story.' Jemmy could no longer hold her bladder and when the warm wetness spread down her leg, she started to cry.

'Oh my goodness, she's really upset. Who was the mannie, pet?' Flora knelt by her daughter's side.

'God's sake, girl. What a load of shite.' Jock pulled himself to his feet and set the ball of twine and the needle to one side. 'Come on, Thomas,' he said to the man seated at the other side of the fireplace. Let's go and take a look.'

'No need for you to go with your bad back,' Thomas said springing to his feet. 'I'll go. I'll come back and let you know if there's anything to tell.'

'Will Reeva come and get me if she knows I told?' Jemmy clutched at her mother as a new wave of terror gripped her.

'No, no, no. I'm sure it's no what it seems.' Flora straightened up and went to the window. 'I'll have a word with Malcolm. Frightening a bairn that's just lost her dad isna' very funny. I swear he'll be giving ye nightmares. We'll have a wee drop tea.'

'But I saw her, too.'

'Thomas'll get to the bottom of it. Ye'll be wrong.'

Flora made the tea and pressed a cup into her daughter's hands. It was too sweet and too milky, but Jemmy drank it anyway.

When Thomas returned he shook his head. 'There's nothing on the beach but a bundle of old clothes,' he said. 'That's likely what ye saw, her throwing away some old clothes.'

Jemmy didn't want to argue. Nobody argued in front of Grandad

'See?' said Flora. 'Ye've got it wrong, love. Come away and finish yer tea.'

Jemmy sniffed and lowered her voice. 'I didn't get it wrong.' She knew what she'd seen. 'Ask Malcolm. He saw it, too.'

'I'll away to have words with that lad tonight, mark my words.' Grandad's gruff voice boomed across the room.

'Dinna be wild with him. We both saw it,' insisted Jemmy.

'I'll speak to the lad,' said Thomas, quietly.

'Hmmph,' was Grandad's reply, and he took a seat at the table.

'I won't stay,' said Thomas. 'I've remembered something I need to do.'

His face was whiter than usual and he looked angry.

Jemmy wondered if it was her fault.

'Are ye sure?' said Flora. 'I've made enough.'

'Aye, I'll come back tomorrow. And you, don't worry about a thing.' Thomas smiled and set his hand on Jemmy's head, and suddenly her world was all right again.

'Here you go.'

Jemmy watched as her mother set the bowl of broth before her grandad. He rubbed his hands together and the rough skin made a papery noise. In the corner, the wireless crackled out its news, to which Jemmy paid little attention. Granddad, however, seemed to have his ear pressed to the contraption at every available opportunity. Even now he cocked his head as if to catch every word.

'Did you move the sheep to the top field yet, Dad?' asked Flora. 'Listening to the news every hour won't make any difference and the work still needs to be done. I can't do everything.'

He shook his head. 'I'm getting too old for the croft.' Picking up his spoon he stretched his wizened neck, pulling an aggrieved face as he did so. 'We need a man to run things. My back pained me something terrible last night. Didn't get a wink of sleep.' He cleared his throat and made a hmmph-hmm noise.

'Jemmy, time for your tea,' Flora shouted to the girl who sat in the window seat.

Jemmy set aside the book she had been pretending to read while listening to the adult's conversation.

Flora returned to the table and lifted her slice of the thickly-cut loaf. 'Wash your hands, Jemmy,' she said. 'There's clean water in the basin.'

Jock cleared his throat again. 'Ye'll need to get married again, Flora, a grand-looking lassie like you. Why don't you take Thomas? He's a fine man.' He raised the spoon to his lips and slurped loudly, something that always annoyed Jemmy.

'I like him fine enough, but I've told you before that I'll not get married just because you need a hand and my man no yet cold in his grave. And wheest in front of the bairn.' Flora's voice dropped as Jemmy took her place at the table. 'And anyway,' she added, 'what do we really know about Thomas? He's only been here a couple of years.'

Jock MacKenzie tore off a chunk of bread and dipped it in his soup. 'See any more men getting thrown off cliffs?' he asked Jemmy when she took her seat across from him.

Jemmy felt her face grow hot and she stared at the table, wishing her grandfather would stop making fun of her. That he didn't believe her was obvious, but his constant referring to what he called her 'overactive imagination' annoyed her. She knew what she had seen, but she wished she'd never mentioned it.

'Don't make fun of her,' said Flora. 'Of course, she must have been mistaken, but to her, it's real enough.'

Jemmy lifted her head and glowered at her grandfather.

'Don't mind him, pet. Now finish your soup like a good lassie and you can go and play for another hour.' She sighed, looked at Jock and shook her head. 'I wish you wouldn't.'

'That bairn's too touchy for her own good. And cheeky. Children should be seen but not heard.' Jock pointed his spoon at Flora. 'It's a hard life this. You need to be tougher on her. I'm telling you, you're making a rod for your own back.'

'She's a wee bit sensitive that's all.'

Jemmy pressed her chin to her chest. Granddad only wanted what was best for her, so Mam said, but Jemmy believed he would have liked her better had she been a boy. She'd overheard him once say that women were only good for one thing, whatever that was. He had gone on to say that a man needed a son to run the croft after his days.

'Just try to stop taking everything to heart,' Mam whispered as she knelt to lift the plates.

Jemmy raised her eyes and through the window, she glimpsed Thomas Bartley striding towards the house, his copper hair scraped back under his cap, his face serious.

'Thomas has come back, Mam,' said Jemmy with an exclamation of glee.

'Oh,' Flora said. 'Now, Dad, don't you dare say anything to shame me. We're no more than friends, and neither of us wants more.'

'Whatever you say, lassie.'

Thomas opened the door and came in through the narrow, dark passageway. Jemmy, with a yell, slipped from the table and ran to meet him. As he entered the kitchen, he swung her up and off her feet.

'Again, Thomas, again,' she shrieked, giggling.

'Leave the man alone. It'll no be you he's come to see.' Jock's raised voice brooked no argument, and Jemmy immediately dropped to the ground clutching her hands to her side, her smile fading.

'Och, the lass is fine.' Thomas ruffled her hair. 'Aren't you, pet?'

She nodded, keeping her head lowered. How she wished her mam would marry Thomas. He'd never take her dad's place, but Jemmy wouldn't mind Mam getting married again as long as it was to someone nice. Thomas'd be a lovely stepdad and maybe a buffer between her and her granddad, who always seemed cross these days.

'Flora, get a wee dram for this man,' Granda' said.

Mam went to the back porch and returned with two glasses of what always made Jemmy think of pee.

'There you go.'

'Looks like the war is imminent,' said Grandad, between puffs as he lit his pipe.

'Come on, pet, we'll leave the men to their business,' Flora said. 'We'll away and do the milking.' And her mam ushered her out the door.

Dolly the cow turned her mournful face towards them as they entered the byre, snorted, flattened her ears and whisked her tail.

'I know I'm late, girl,' said Flora, pulling the milking stool into place. 'You'll soon feel better now.'

Jemmy stared at the meagre trickle Dolly produced.

'She's an old cow and she's not giving milk the way she should,' said Mam, wearily.

'Will I have to go to Annabel's for more?' Jemmy asked, the sudden fear of leaving the safety of her home gripping her anew.

'Let's see what we can get,' said Flora.

'Mam, is there going to be a war?' Jemmy asked as the milk hit the pail with a tinny resonance.

Flora was quiet for a beat. 'There might be.'

'Like last time?' Jemmy had heard the grown-ups talk of the war and their stories had scared her. Her dad had come back a different man and suffered bouts of despair ever since. Grandad had not been too careful with what he said in front of Jemmy, although Mam was always giving him a row for it. But then Jemmy had been born thirteen years after the war and hadn't known her dad any other way.

'I hope it won't come to that.' But Flora's voice was tense, and Jemmy shivered.

'Flora, can I have a word with you?' came a voice from the door, startling both woman and child. Jemmy looked up to see Thomas standing there, a dark shadow against the light from beyond.

'Of course, you can. It's good you came back.' Flora straightened up. 'Jock enjoys your company.'

'And I enjoy his. And yours, too.' As he spoke, his eyes slipped from hers to Jemmy's.

'Jemmy, would you mind playing outside for a little while? I need to speak to your mam in private.'

Jemmy bit back her disappointment. She was fond of Thomas

and wanted him to swing her into the air as he often did, but he looked drawn, worried.

'But I wanted to play,' she said.

'Maybe a wee while later.' Thomas wasn't looking at her, he was looking at her mam.

'Promise?'

'I promise.'

She pouted and hung her head, but went outside anyway. Thomas shut the door, and their voices dropped to little more than a murmur.

She scraped her foot in the dry earth. If there was a war, maybe Thomas would have to go away and fight. Maybe he would come back changed like Daddy did, or maybe he wouldn't come back at all. She could hardly bear the thought.

When Thomas came out of the barn, his face was grim. Although he smiled at her, Jemmy didn't feel there was any happiness there.

'Your Mam wants to speak to you,' he said, his face serious. 'You pay heed to her, mind.' And he strode down the path.

She stared after him. It didn't look like he was going to keep his promise and play with her, but by now the excitement had grown thin.

Flora came out of the byre, her face as serious as Thomas's had been. She knelt down before Jemmy. 'Now listen,' she said, her voice low. 'What you saw Reeva push off the cliff was a bunch of clothes, nothing else. And you've got to forget all about it. Don't speak about it in school or anywhere else, you hear me?'

'Yes, but...'

Flora's voice rose a notch. 'This is very important, Jemmy.'

'You mean it's a secret?'

'Yes, yes, that's it. It's a very big secret. Now promise me you'll not speak about it again, not even to Malcolm.'

Jemmy couldn't understand why she couldn't speak about it to Malcolm, but her mam looked scared, and that scared her.

'Promise me,' said Flora, more forcefully.

'I...I,,,promise.' Jemmy's voice trembled. Mam's grip on her arm was hurting. 'Will she kill us?' she asked, sure there was a real danger. There must be, to make her mam act like this.

'No, of course not,' said Flora. 'But there are some bad people out there. I don't want you to be scared, love, but you mustn't speak about this ever again and we'll be fine. Now come away in and say nothing to your granddad.'

'But he keeps going on about it, Mam.'

'He won't any more. He'll make his own tea if he does!' She gave a nervous laugh, and Jemmy giggled, the tension of a moment ago almost forgotten. Yet a little knot of worry stayed inside her. There was something going on, and she didn't like not knowing what it was.

***

Thomas Bartley licked dry lips. Now, at last, under the cover of darkness could he get this sorted. Things often went wrong, but this! He only hoped he'd scared Flora enough that she would make sure Jemmy kept her mouth shut, otherwise, he did not want to contemplate the consequences. Malcolm was older, and more definite in what he saw. He might pose a bigger problem.

With no light other than a sporadic moon, he dodged from one clump of bushes to the next and silently cursed the lack of trees in Caithness. Although he'd been resident here for over two years, he was not well acquainted with the terrain on this hill.

The cottage was a darker shadow among shadows and only a faint sliver of light showed between black, drawn curtains. He gave three sharp taps on the door.

'Thomas,' a voice whispered. 'Is that you?' and there was a click as the door was unlocked.

He stood in the glare from a triumphant moon suddenly free from cloud cover, and quickly stepped into the house, shutting the door behind him. Standing erect and without her long, grey wig, Reeva looked a very different person, almost attractive, the ghost of the girl she once was still in her features.

'What the hell happened?' he asked, as he followed her into the kitchen, the dazzle of light from the tilly lamp momentarily blinding him.

Reeva took a deep breath. 'He found the radio. He attacked me.' Her face was granite hard, showing no emotion.

'But throwing him off the cliff? Are you mad, woman?'

'Do you think I did it deliberately?' She shook her head. 'He was cleverer than we suspected, more cunning. He meant to throw me off the cliff. "They'll think you killed yourself," he said. "They all think you're mad anyway."'

'This is a disaster. He had so much information we could have gotten out of him. But how did you —'

'All those self-defence lessons came in handy,' Reeva said. 'Physically stronger than me, he thought he had me, and then…and then… it was me or him. He fell and lost his footing. I know this is a disaster, but it was me or him. Did anyone see?'

'A couple of kids. I volunteered to look.' He held up his hand as she started to speak again. 'Don't worry, I went alone. The body's well hidden.'

'But the kids. We'll have to shut them up.'

'No one believes them. I've convinced them it was just a bundle of old clothes.'

'But if the story gets to the right ears, someone may put two and two together. If there was one spy in the area, there may be more.'

'I think I've taken care of it.'

'Think…Think?' her voice rose. 'Thinking's not good enough. What are we going to do?'

'You'll have to move on. Get out of here.'

'I gathered that. But will that be enough? This is too important.'

'I've spoken to the parents—'

'What?' She turned cold, steel eyes on him.

'I didn't tell them anything important. Look, I've lived with these people, I know them. I'll sort everything.'

'Don't tell me you're going soft? I've no wish to harm an innocent party, especially children, but we don't dare risk the operation being put in danger.' She went to a box and withdrew a vial. 'Here, a few drops in a cup of tea and they'll feel nothing.' She held it out to him.

When he hesitated, she carried on, 'Think how many more will be killed if this gets out? Yes, okay, it was my fault, I should have taken more care of my prisoner, but in view of what happened, there is bound to be damage. If you're totally committed to the cause, moving me to another location, talking to the adults, do you really think that's enough? Listen to yourself. You've grown too close to the locals, and that could prove to be your Achilles' Heel.'

He felt the sweat bead on his brow and thought of the evidence he had already gathered.

'Just get everything together,' Thomas said grimly, and took the vial from her.

'Where am I going?'

'The less you know at this stage the better,' was the reply. 'Hell, I don't even know. You've got a couple of hours to get the stuff packed up, then I'll come for you.'

'Thomas,' she grabbed his arm. 'If they find out it's us feeding them information instead of their spy, it could change everything. You know that.'

Two hours. A few loose ends and he knew their work was done here.

Reeva was right about one thing, he had grown too soft for this job, but not too soft for what he had to do.

'Two hours.' He turned and walked into the dark. Surely they'd done enough to ward off the seaborne landing on the north coast of Scotland. The naval base on Scapa Flow had already been reinforced. He weighed the vial in his hand his heart heavy at what was to come.

On the gentle breeze, the scent of heather and sea was strong. His life could have been so different. For a short time, he had thought it still might be. Flora and her family would never know how much they had come to mean to him.

In the predawn, he could see the outline of the cottage where she lived with her father and daughter and his heart ached. He fingered the vial in his pocket.

Too soon, the two hours were up. He had to return to Reeva or her suspicions would be aroused. He slipped silently into the stillness of the blacked-out cottage.

'Well?' came her disembodied voice. She sat bolt upright at the table, her dishevelment backlit by a stubby candle on the dresser, an undrunk cup of tea at her elbow, a smattering of boxes at her feet.

Thomas nodded. 'I will take care of it, have no fear of that,' he said in as steady a voice as he could manage.

'Excellent.'

'I'm dry,' he said. 'Get me a cup of tea before we go.'

She rose and went towards the sink.

As soon as her back was turned, Thomas tipped half the contents of the vial into her tea.

She returned, poured him a cup and, with their mugs, they toasted each other on a job completed.

Reeva lifted her cup to her lips.

Thomas watched as those lips slowly formed a rictus grin.

Her cup clattered to the flagstone floor.

She fell after it, twitching and writhing as the strychnine did its deadly work.

Thomas wondered how much damage had already been done.

'Why, Reeva? Did you think we wouldn't find out? ' he said sadly. 'You will be no more use to your Nazi masters now!'

He walked to the door, opened it and breathed in the clear morning air. A slash of light severed the horizon to the north. There was no more time for reflection, no more time for regrets.

To Tell or Not to Tell

by Morag Anderson

Strictly was on the telly, the fire was burning brightly and the dogs were curled up sleeping. All was quiet as I settled down for the evening. It should have been the perfect Saturday night but somehow it did not feel right. A growing sense of unease pervaded me as if somebody was trying to tell me something. The air felt different, disconcerting. Doug, the old collie, gave a rumbling growl in his throat making the hairs on the back of my neck stand up. *Not going to settle now*, I thought.

On impulse, I decided to ring Mysie, my neighbour and lifelong friend. I was a bit worried, she had not been her usual cheerful self lately. This afternoon she had been fidgety, complaining of a headache and just out of sorts, so unlike her as she was not one to moan.

The phone rang and rang. Worried now, I grabbed my torch and took the well-worn path between her house and mine. As I got closer I noticed her house was in darkness. Very odd.

'Mysie, Mysie, it's me,' I called as I made my way to the kitchen switching the lights on as I went.

I found her lying on the floor in a puddle of blood, looking as if she had toppled off her chair, catching the side of her head on the corner of the fireplace.

Mysie and I have been friends and soul mates since the day we were born. We started school on the same day. That first day and for the next forty years, we held hands. We had an ESP all of our own even finishing each other's sentences. Every up and down in life, we weathered together. We both married young. Mysie could have had her pick of every handsome man that crossed her path; she was sensationally beautiful. In the end, she chose Phil, a charismatic rogue, but I saw through him. I begged her and pleaded with her, but still, she went ahead.

At first, I ignored the bruises, the cuts, and the days she would not leave the house. But when, after one more unprovoked attack, she lost her baby, that was the final straw. By this time Phil had found someone younger, richer and prettier, but even so, he did not leave willingly, preferring to have his cake and eat it.

Eventually, Paul, my strong, steadfast husband intervened, persuading him of the error of his ways. That was a difficult time but together we weathered it. It made us stronger and even closer than ever. Or so I thought. Was this when it happened?

Paul died last year, forty years of happy marriage, barely a cross word. I was devastated. If it wasn't for Mysie, I would not be here to tell the tale. Many a night she sat with me, holding my hand, talking as we shed tears together. She was as broken-hearted as I was, but now, one year on, I feel able to tackle the mammoth job of packing his clothes, selling his tools and all the paraphernalia he accumulated during his life. He was a hoarder; I don't think he threw out anything in forty years. She offered to help, but I'm so glad now I declined this offer.

I collected her when she was released from the hospital — shortage of beds they said. I took her home. The stroke, coupled with the head wound was pretty bad but I looked after her, together we would manage. I was sure that somewhere inside, she was still the same Mysie. She looked at me, willing me to understand. We always managed without words and now was no different.

It wasn't how life was supposed to be. We were in our golden years, a time to slow down and enjoy what time we had left. Now it was all bed pans, feeding, and washing—she needed me for everything. I didn't mind; I loved her so much.

Today I started to clear out. The memories flooded back. All the years of companionship, all the achievements, all the holidays all the photographs, the three of us, a complete life together. Boxes, boxes, so many boxes.

The one under the bed was different. I dragged it out, lifted the lid, and was assailed by her perfume. I would recognize it anywhere. My curiosity was piqued, what was this? My heart thudded with a growing sense of foreboding as picked up the first envelope.

Time, they say, heals everything. In time, they say, you can forgive and forget. There were many letters in the box, twenty-five years of letters. Her writing was quite distinctive. Another thing I easily recognised.

My dearest Paul, the love of my life. On and on they went. My husband and my best friend, lovers for twenty-five years. How can this be possible, my honest, transparent husband and my best friend in the whole world? How? Well, they say, do you know the person closest to you.

She lay in her bed and I knew without me there she would remain. The sense of betrayal was deep. My sense of duty was equally powerful. I needed to wash Mysie's beautiful hair, I needed to feed her. Did she know? Could she tell? I looked her in the eye, willing her to speak. There were questions I wanted to ask. *Why did you do it*? Why Paul when you had your choice of all the men you desired? But then I got to thinking, *why did Paul do this to me*? Unfortunately, there would never be any answers.

It is a beautiful clear frosty morning as I walk the dogs over the fields. The old collie, on his last legs now, tottering behind, still enjoying the fresh air and all the exciting smells. Mysie is dead now, dead these last six months. She went peacefully in the end, surrounded by the photographs of her life, our life, Paul myself and Mysie. The things we shared, the good times, the bad times and everything in between. Yes, she went peacefully, I never did tell her what I found.

A Stick to Beat My Mother

by John Crofts

'You're mine,' he breathed.

Andrew was an honest man, but he stole the stick without a second thought. He fondled the smooth, hard, wooden handle and pulled it from the wicker basket. It felt at home in his hand. It eased his limp as he tried it out, the metal end clicking loudly on the stone floor of the old manse. An unusual sense of well-being touched his loneliness.

His welcome to the far north of Scotland had been curt.

'You on your own? First guest this spring. Place is still cold. Keep your warm clothes on.'

The hostel manager had shown him into the large hall dominated by an impressive staircase.

'Your bedroom is first upstairs. Looks straight down the valley. You make your own meals and tidy up afterwards.'

The manager opened a door off the side of the hall marked *Private*.

'This is where *I* live.'

And Andrew was on his own. That was when he stole the stick.

That night, he propped the stick against his bed. He looked down the valley to the loch, shining in the starlight. Despite the damp chill of the room, he was surprised at how at peace he felt. Andrew was forty-five but knew he was close to the end of his life. His lungs were shot.

He had been brought up in an orphanage in Glasgow. They had been kind to him, but nobody had ever loved him. He had been farmed out three times but it never lasted. A very lonely man, he had never married and never had what he longed for most—a mother's love.

That was why he was here now. He had survived the orphanage, he had survived working in Glasgow Docks and he had survived the Great War, although it had left him with poor lungs and a limp. Now, in the depression of the nineteen thirties, jobless, poor and without a future, he just wanted to know where he came from before he died.

As he fell asleep, his hand caressed the smooth handle of the stick, now somehow in bed with him.

He woke on the bottom landing of the stairs. The air was icy cold and moonlight flooded the hallway beneath him. From behind the private door, he heard footsteps and tapping. A figure passed through the closed door and limped into the hall, leaning on a worn, dark wooden stick. Andrew could not move.

The man was only middle-aged but the ravages of drink made him look older. He wore black clothes except for the white flash of a minister's collar at his neck.

A baby's cry broke the frozen silence and the man, muttering angrily, hurried into the front room. Andrew followed. A woman lay on the settee, holding a newborn baby squirming and crying in her arms. The minister was beating her with his stick. She appeared too weak to move but hunched over the baby to shield it from the blows. A maid stood in the corner, cowering with fear.

'Harlot. Whore,' the Minister shouted. Tempered by drink his blows were not hard or accurate.

The woman looked up at him and whimpered. 'Call yourself a man of God! What sort of father are you?'

As she spoke, the blows cut across her now upturned face. The crimson blood gushed from her opened cheek as she bent her face down to the baby again. She sobbed in agony as the minister beat her again and then turned on his heel and hobbled out through the door.

The click of the garden gate beneath his window woke Andrew, clammy with sweat in his already damp bed. The gate clicked again and he heard hurried footsteps and the tapping of a stick, but by the time he got out of bed and opened the curtain, there was nothing to see.

That morning, Andrew walked down the valley to the loch, his stolen stick helping him on the stony track. His dream had unnerved him, but for some reason, he had an unusual feeling of well-being.

'Because it's spring,' he thought.

Just before the loch, the track rose over a stone bridge that crossed the burn. Beneath it, the water crashed twenty feet down a waterfall into the deep grey loch. He felt neither the weak spring sunshine on his back nor the cold wind biting his cheeks as he stared down at it, lost in the noise and deep in thought.

He had been brought to the orphanage in 1888.

'From up north,' he had been told.

'That's all we know. Go ask the police. They brought you.'

So he had. And months later he had ended up here on nothing more than somebody's memory of a baby abandoned in these hills and a story of a housemaid finding the child. The mother and father had drowned. The dates were vague but it fit his age. Now he was here and there was nobody to ask. He stared at the water and for the first time in years, he felt at peace.

That night Andrew slept well but he woke in the first glimmer of grey morning light. Once more it was a noise that woke him. The careful closing of the front door, footsteps down the gravel path and then the grating of the gate.

This time he rose from his bed and pulled aside his curtains in time to see the dark-eyed mother hurrying down the path to the loch, shielding her baby under her shawl. As he watched her, she paused and looked back at the house. She stared up at his window, at him, and caught his eye, as if begging him to come with her. Then she turned and scurried on.

The front door opened again, this time much less carefully.

'Kirsten.' A long plaintive cry travelled down the valley after her.

'For God's sake Kirsten. Come back woman.'

And then more quietly, 'I'm Sorry. I'm so sorry.' But she didn't seem to hear any of it.

Black boots crunched over the gravel, accompanied by the furious tapping of a stick as the minister hobbled after Kirsten. He was through the gate and gone before Andrew pulled on his boots.

He grasped the smooth handle of the stolen walking stick and limped down the stairs and through the open doors into the cold dawn. He strained to listen but heard nothing above the rushing of the wind.

This time it was no dream as he stumbled the half-mile along the stony track to the bridge and the loch, his sick lungs burning and his pulse pounding in his temples. The dawn was passing to full daylight by the time the bridge came into sight. What he saw brought him to a halt. The woman was balanced on the bridge parapet, still clutching the baby. The minister stumbled towards her, one arm stretched out imploringly and only yards away from being able to clutch at her flying skirts.

'Kirsten. For pity's sake don't.'

She said not a word as she looked back. But it was Andrew she looked at, not the minister. He saw again the open wound across her cheek, the flattened and bruised nose, the split lip, blackened with clotted blood, and the black bruise around one eye. She held his gaze until the minister grasped her flailing skirts and then she jumped off the edge and into the waterfall, still clutching her baby. Her skirts slipped easily from the minister's grasp and she was gone.

Andrew watched helplessly as the minister dropped his stick, climbed onto the parapet, swayed to and fro for a few seconds and then plunged down into the water after his wife and baby.

Suddenly all was quiet except for the crashing of the waterfall. Andrew found his legs and stumbled down past the bridge to the edge of the loch, the water whipped by the wind but empty, cold and grey.

'Kirsten,' he shouted and then again, but longer, 'Kirsten.'

There was a struggling in the water and Kirsten appeared, gasping for breath, water pouring from her sodden clothes and hair. She crawled on her knees in the shallows pushing her bundle in front of her. She had enough strength to push the bundle, dripping, sodden and bellowing, onto the bank above her. Then she slipped back into the water and drifted away.

Andrew heard a clattering of stones on the track far behind him. Two figures were running to the bridge, the hostel manager and the minister's maid. They both looked at the loch and shouted, but he couldn't make out the words. He turned back to the water where the mass of skirts were still floating, just out of reach.

'Mother,' he said, and then louder, 'Mother. I'm here Mother.'

Kirsten rose up until her head and shoulders were out of the water. She looked at Andrew, smiled and held out her arms to him. He stepped into the water and walked forward until it was up to his waist, and held out his stick.

'Here Mother. Take hold. I'll pull you out.'

She smiled again, grasped the shiny handle, but continued to walk backwards away from him. He pulled at first but then followed her meekly into the loch. As the water lapped over his head she wrapped him in her arms.

'I heard him go out,' the hostel manager told the policeman in the front room of the house. 'I ran after him. Shouted to him. But the idiot just walked into the water with a stupid smile on his face. Took my bloody walking stick with him, too. Had that for years, I have. Came with the house.'

'I heard them run out,' the maid said, when it was her turn to give evidence. 'When I got down to the loch there was no sign of them, just this poor little soul, soaking and crying for his Mother. I guess he'll never see her again.' She handed over the now dry, but still crying, bundle. She put the stick she had found on the bridge back in the basket in the hall.

Accordion Afternoon

by Sharon Gunason Pottinger

For JG with many thanks

a not quite spring afternoon
a pale sun warming the air
cold lingering in the earth
clouds stretching in pale layers
like fresh-washed sheets on the horizon
everything still and slow and hollow
the accordion breathed itself into life
waltzes and memory and promises
of seasons to come filled the empty spaces
and the blackbird sang along
and the geese in their skeins
wound homeward in the twilight

Harbour Lights

by Jean MacLennan

The weather matched my mood. The air was sliced by a cutting wind, scouring my face. Litter, tumbleweed and thick dust swirled in corners. The sea and sky shared the same shade of dark grey. Only a hardy few folk bent into the gale heading homeward if they were wise. I hardly glanced at the view over the harbour and river. I'd been dreading this meeting and wouldn't be here if it hadn't been for Becca's insistence it was something I needed to do, to let me move on. I would not have taken in much of my surroundings but my mind was looking for anything to divert my attention from what potentially lay ahead for me this evening.

It seemed the man I was meeting shared my preference for taverns that could have metamorphosed out of hidden drinking dens from times of temperance, with only a little respectability now they were legitimate. Harbour Lights looked suitably unprepossessing from the outside to make it onto my list of favourite inns. Small dark windows streaked with dirt, high in the walls, would let in little natural light even had it been daytime. Around them, scabby paintwork included a name sign so faded, bleached by the sun, as to be just, only just, legible. I hesitated on the threshold listening and was delighted there was no music, either of the musak variety or from whatever the modern-day equivalent of jukeboxes might spew out. Lino tiles scuffed to a dirty, amorphous grey led to a solid, wooden, handleless door. It swung readily to admit me.

Inside was gloomy, as if one of those long-life bulbs had just been lit and was still warming up. This dingy impression was reinforced by dark wood fixtures topped by plaster walls of a hue suggesting the nicotine of generations of heavy smokers. Freshness in the atmosphere now confirmed rigorous cleaning with no bending of the no smoking indoors rules.

A small gantry was set behind a dark wood counter that gleamed as if it had been burnished by the sleeves of thousands of past customers. The barmaid, a woman with big, blonde hair and a slash of deep crimson lipstick on her narrow lips was busy buffing a pint glass. She treated me to an open-mouthed, toothy smile that made me think of a shark, but she seemed friendly enough and there was always the counter between us.

The bar was empty but for the two of us. Was it always as quiet as this? I noticed a small, open fire in a corner to the left and felt drawn to it. I slid onto a chair at the end of the bar and let the welcome heat sink into my back. The woman had watched my progress and now she raised her eyebrows and reached a hand towards the glasses held in racks above.

'Pint?'

'And a chaser. Whatever whisky you've got.'

A rush of cold air heralded the arrival of another customer. I glanced round to see an exchange of nods after which the newcomer tilted his head towards me. The woman shook her head at him. Conversation wasn't high on the agenda in Harbour Lights, and that suited me fine. I was rehearsing, for the umpteenth time, the words I was saving and would say when the man I was waiting for arrived.

The newcomer propped his elbows on the counter and leant forward. He was short, about five three, small built, in his sixties wearing a nondescript brown jacket over jeans and brown loafers. I couldn't hear the muffled conversation but I guessed it was about me from the look both participants gave me with the last words spoken. Strangers were obviously a rare species here.

'It's OK,' she told him at normal volume.

Wednesday night wasn't a busy night in my fairly extensive experience of small-town pubs. Those customers dependent on benefits were waiting for their money and it wasn't pay day for the weekly paid. This pub was no exception. by ten o'clock only six men were supping their drinks. I had drawn some glances but the only conversation had been with Patsy. She'd revealed her name as I ordered my second pint.

Closing time was still some way off but I was checking my watch every few minutes. Where was he? I'd come a long way for this. It was to be my last chance to find some kind of peace. Becca had persuaded me to write a letter. Then when I got no response, to make the journey north. All kinds of emotions, mainly anger with a topping of bitterness had simmered in me for many years, boiling up when I held our son, James. On his third birthday even as I was filled with love for my boy, watching him play with his new toys I felt the loss, what I had missed in my own past, the love and life I should have had. With adulthood, those feelings had been always there, in the background.

'You need to go and sort this out,' said my lovely wife. 'You need to put the past behind you, one way or the other.' Auntie Mags said he came here every evening. I thought Harbour Lights was neutral territory, safer. Whether this was safer for me or for him was something I chose not to dwell on. I didn't know how either of us were going to react. So this was where I had chosen for a possible confrontation.

I was aware of Patsy watching me, as I was checking the time yet again.

'Got somewhere to go?' she asked. I shook my head.

'You aren't local?' she asked.

I took a short moment before answering. Should I mention my early childhood here? After all I hadn't grown up here nor lived here as an adult and the only person I'd had any contact with here was Auntie Mags, and she was dead now. I decided not. 'Edinburgh. Here for a short break.'

'Not the best time for a holiday. It's bloody cold right now.'

I had to agree with that. She brought a shuttle of coal round the end of the counter and I took it from her and tossed some of its contents onto the fire. I felt six sets of eyes boring into me and there was a muttered exchange among the other drinkers as I handed the shuttle back.

'You planning to be back tomorrow?' she asked.

'Don't think so. I might head back to Edinburgh. Nothing to keep me here.'

'It's just that we're closed tomorrow. Private party. One of the regulars died last week. It's his chair you've been sitting on all night.' Her words gave me the strangest feeling like a cold hand reaching down my back. I felt myself shudder.

'What was his name?'

'Eneus Gunn. Why?'

'I came to meet him here. I knew this was his local. What happened?'

'Heart attack they said. No warning. He was always here. Every night without fail. He didn't come in last Friday so I went round to his house to see he was all right. He was sitting dead in his chair. I could see that through his window. I got the police and they broke in.' She stopped the flow of words and looked harder at my face.

'Oh, my God. It's you, isn't it. His son. And you've been sitting there, on his chair all night, and not knowing.' Shock raised her voice and I was aware her words caught the attention of the other pub goers.

I don't know how I felt, hearing he was dead. It wasn't as if I'd had a relationship with him. Yes, he was my father, but he'd nothing to do with me for over thirty years. And it was his fault my mother was dead. I was struggling to sort out my feelings at the news when the man sitting closest to me, the one who'd arrived just after me, having overheard Patsy's words, came over. He grasped my hand without me offering and shook it. Concern was drawn over his features.

'I'm Andy. Eneus was my friend, and he was a good man. Ask anyone here,' he said, sweeping an arm around, taking in the other drinkers who were now all caught up in the drama as it unfolded. They were watching, nodding, agreeing with his words. Patsy, unasked, laid a large whisky in front of me.

'Aye. Your dad was a good man. We all know what happened all those years ago. This is a small town, and there are long memories.' She hesitated, took a breath. 'You poor soul, losing your Mum like that.' She paused again. 'He regretted it, every day. If anyone ever paid for doing something wrong, then he did. in spades. He accepted it was all his fault. No excuses, never any excuses. He'd sit there every night, drinking. Yes, drinking. But no alcohol. He was very careful about that. And the number of men he has helped quietly, in his own way, to stop them from going down the same road. Sharing his story, his grief for your mum, and for you too. He said he didn't deserve you, and you were better off without him.'

'Tomorrow, lad,' said Andy, 'it'll be hard, but maybe you could come to the cemetery. You'll see how well he was thought of.' I was still trying to come to terms with the news I'd been given. Auntie Mags had written about him visiting my Mum's grave often. She wrote of him sitting on a bench nearby in all weathers; of him taking flowers, tending the grave.

Once Mum had taken her own life there was no going back, and Social Services had decided, as an alcoholic, my father wasn't a fit person to have care of three-year-old me. I didn't know if Auntie Mags was exaggerating how penitent he was in an attempt to mollify me. I still had a question, but would anyone know the answer?

'I wrote to him recently. He didn't reply,' I said to Andy.

'He was never one for letters. He was talking about visiting Edinburgh in a couple of weeks. He was going to come and see you. And here you are.'

As I arrived at Harbour Lights that night I was angry and bitter, ready for a confrontation if that was what happened. As Patsy closed the door behind me when I stepped outside I realised the wind had dropped. The moon shone brightly, and I looked down on boats dancing in the ever-moving water. I felt as if the lights of the harbour were wiping away many of my negative feelings. A new sense of peace about my past was settling over me.

I dialled home. 'Becca, I'm going to stay another couple of days.'

'What happened? You sound …I was going to say, happy.'

'It's OK. It's late now. I'm tired. It's been a stressful experience. I should have come sooner, but better late than never. I'll phone tomorrow and tell you everything that's happened. It's a long story. I'm still processing it myself. Love you and James. Tell him Daddy will be home soon and give him a big hug for me. And one for yourself too. And Becca, you were right. I needed to be here.'

The River Bank

by Irena Bracey

The book was found in a charity shop in Devon. by the state of the pages, it looked like the reader gave up halfway through. Grubby finger marks at the beginning but the other half looked untouched. The inscription on the inside cover read:

To Arthur, age 9
For doing well in your exams
From Mum and Dad xx

Arthur didn't like school. He didn't hate it but he struggled, so he was surprised when his teacher read out the marks for the end-of-year exams. You could even say he was baffled by the results- he was in the top five of his class! His best friend, Gordy, was also amazed and gave Arthur a well-deserved pat on the back. Gordy, on the other hand, loved school. Arithmetic was his favourite subject and the tuition he gave Arthur had paid off. Arthur couldn't wait to tell his parents who would be shocked but pleased. This had been a particularly good day because Arthur scored a goal in the lunchtime game of football. He was usually a reserve but when Jimmy twisted his ankle, he took his place. The ball came towards him and he just kicked it. The goalie was obviously not prepared for this from the sub and was caught off guard. A fluke, maybe, but he grinned from ear to ear all afternoon. One of his better days and to top it off the summer holidays started tomorrow.

Two days later there was a book lying on the table. His mother told him to open it. Pleased when he read the inscription, he thanked her and said he would start reading *The Wind in the Willows* when he'd finished his new comic. Meanwhile, he put it away in the box he kept under his bed for special things.

It was five years since the end of the war. Arthur's first home, which he doesn't remember, had been bombed and the family were now renting a flat above a greengrocer. His father had a good job in the car plant on the outskirts of town, their slogan was 'Building Britain Back'. His mother, a nurse, was pregnant so would soon have to give up her job, which would make saving to buy somewhere even harder.

'Had a letter from Aunty Joan, Arthur.' His mother said the next morning. 'She's looking forward to seeing you soon now that school has finished.'

Joan was his mother's older, unmarried sister who lived in Devon. Joan's fiancé had been a pilot. His plane was shot down over France and he died before they were able to bring him back to England. She decided she needed a change of scenery from the bombed buildings, which were reminders of her loss and that of many like her. Besides, the dust from the rubble in the town was making her asthma worse. She soon became involved in the life of a small village outside Torquay where she found a job in the local shop and post office. Arthur loved staying with her during his holidays and never wanted to go back to a busy town. He told everyone that he was going to live in Devon when he was old enough.

'Can Gordy come with me this year, Mum?' he asked looking up from his cornflakes.

'I'll speak to Sylvie. She'll be happy for him to get some sea air, I should think.'

It was agreed that both boys would take the train to Torquay in a couple of days. Arthur put his new book in his new suitcase amongst the clothes his mother had packed for him. She always put in a gift for her sister, this year a brooch in the shape of a shell and some spending money for Arthur. He also had a bag of fruit, which the greengrocer had given his mother for Joan. Mr Jenkins, the postman, who was also a good friend of Joan's, offered to meet them at the station and drive them to the cottage.

Aunty Joan was delighted to welcome both boys. She told them they would be sharing a room and that there would be freshly baked scones and tea waiting for them downstairs once they'd sorted themselves out upstairs.

Arthur was looking forward to showing his friend all his favourite haunts and the river, all of which were nearby. As the days went by they spent most of their time on the banks, regardless of the weather, and Joan knew exactly where to find them at meal times. They made fishing rods from sticks and string, paper boats and generally messed about in or near the water. Once they were in their beds, Arthur would read his new book out loud which triggered their imaginations for the next day's adventures. They were always on the lookout for water rats, moles, old badgers and of course toads. They made up their own stories about the animals and creatures they came across. A couple of times Arthur took the book with him and read another chapter or two while Gordy, listening to every word, would be on the lookout for the creatures he was hearing about. They had studied the pictures so they could identify them. When she saw the state of the book, Aunty Joan suggested they leave it at home. She told them her sister would be disappointed if they didn't look after it.

One day Mr Jenkins helped them put large stones in the water so they could cross to the other side without getting too wet. Gordy found it hard to balance and kept slipping off the stones after several attempts to get across the 'slippery bridge'. The water was low because it hadn't rained for weeks but he managed to get soaked every time he tried.

'You know how to swim, don't you, Gordy?' The boy shook his head.' I taught Arthur last summer. I'll teach you on my next day off. It's important if you're near water. Everyone should be able to swim.'

The storm, a few nights later, brought thunder and lightning and lots and lots of rain. The boys were happy to stay in their beds under the blankets while it raged outside. Aunty Joan came into their room to see if they were alright. She got two very shaky replies as they came up for air and nodded their heads.

'I hope we don't find too much damage in the garden in the morning. You might have to help me clear it, boys. Haven't had a storm like this for a long time.'

As soon as she'd gone the boys dived back under the blankets until it was over.

The next morning all three stared at the mess in the garden. The wind had finally died down and the sun was attempting to come out from behind white clouds. The clearing up would take most of that day and the next. The river had risen a lot and had there been any more rain, would have flooded the bottom of the garden. They could hear the water rushing past the gate as they filled wheelbarrow after wheelbarrow. by the end of the day, the three of them were well and truly exhausted as they fell into bed. Arthur didn't have the energy to read any more of his book before his head hit the pillow. The water hadn't really abated by the next day. It was still high and was flowing at a fast pace. The villagers were out in force helping each other to bring some sort of order to the devastation the freak weather had left behind. The boys had ventured down to the river to try and clear some of the floating debris and because of the roar of the river, they didn't hear Aunty Joan calling them in for lunch. She came through the gate and saw them kneeling and peering over something, engrossed in deep discussion. As she moved towards the pair, she saw that the 'something' was a dead water rat. From the conversation she overheard it transpired that neither had seen a water rat before, dead or alive, and they were trying to decide which of them should pick it up for a good look. She startled them as she called out.

What suddenly occurred after that, happened so quickly and was all of a blur when they were asked to recount it later. The boys jumped back as Joan appeared from nowhere and Gordy's arm caught her and she fell over. She slipped on the wet bank and slid into the river. Trying to regain her balance she slipped again and hit her head on one of the rocks of the 'stone bridge', which was submerged under the water. Both boys ran down to the river and turned her over but the current was so strong and they had trouble pulling her out. They managed to wedge her between two large stones and Gordy held her head while Arthur ran for help. The sight of Aunty Joan floating in the river had frightened him so much that it rendered him almost speechless as he came up to two men, who were working in Joan's neighbour's garden. The bank was muddy and the men found it hard to keep hold of her lifeless body. Someone had called for the ambulance and the light on it was flashing, as they carried her towards it.

Gordy was in shock and immobile in the river when Mr Jenkins came by to see what the commotion was about. He had his waders on and stepped into the filthy river.

'What are you doing sitting in the water, Gordy? You'll freeze to death. Grab hold of me, lad, and I'll pull you out.'

In between sobs, sniffs, shaking of his head and with the encouragement of his rescuer, he finally managed to answer.

'I've killed her, Mr. Jenkins. I didn't mean to knock her into the river…When I got to her she wasn't moving. I held her head but she didn't open her eyes.' Tears were streaming down his muddied face. 'Aunty Joan is dead… and I'm stuck. I can't get this big stone off my foot. I'm afraid I might drown', he sobbed. 'Can you help me?'. The last few words came out in a whisper.

Mr Jenkins dislodged the stone and helped the limping boy up the bank towards the gate. They met Arthur who hadn't been allowed in the ambulance with his Aunt. Gordy couldn't look at his friend. He kept his head down.

'Why can't you walk properly? What's wrong?'

'I'm sorry, Arthur, about Aunty Joan. I didn't mean to kill her. It was an accident. She startled me and she ended up in the water…'

'What *are* you talking about? You haven't killed anyone. She's not dead, Gordy. The ambulance man said you saved her. You're a hero!'

Gordy looked up and saw that Arthur was smiling.

'She's not dead?' he asked in disbelief.

'No. Don't know what they did but they managed to wake her up and then she was sick. A lot. It was disgusting. I couldn't look. It was worse than when Jack was sick after eating those berries, d'you remember? The man said she was unconscious and keeping her head out of the water, saved her.' He patted his pal on the back.

They didn't notice but there was a look of relief on Mr. Jenkin's face too. 'She's tougher than she looks, is Joan.'

Aunty Joan recovered but the swelling from the bump on her head didn't go away. She had bad headaches and her vision wasn't so good. The stuffing had been knocked out of her but she never let the boys know how she was really feeling. Frequent visits to the doctor and stays in hospital were her new regime. Her sister would come and stay to look after her when she could and Joan's new niece brought a bit of joy.

The funeral, two years later, was well attended. She was well-liked in the village and was sadly missed, especially by Mr. Jenkins, the postman.

She bequeathed her cottage to Arthur who holidayed there with his family until he was old enough to live on his own.

Arthur never finished reading 'Wind in the Willows'. Neither did Gordy. The memories of that holiday stayed with them for a long time and they gave up on Mr. Ratty and his friends. The book was found among many others when Arthur renovated the cottage, and was given to the charity shop in the village, when he was clearing it out.

Gordy learnt to swim and for many years volunteered for the RNLI.

The river, which had caused such mayhem, continued to be a source of pleasure for both young and old. The level of water rose and fell according to the rainfall but it never again rose as high or caused as much damage as in the summer of 1950.

My Voice

by Meg Macleod

my voice is in my fingers
in the touch that affirms
my hands poised Durer fashion
scripted in prayers
a song I do not sing
woven in threads
to keep you warm

an undertone in the earth
can you hear it?

What is Reality

by Alan Sinclair

Gail was the latest in a string of girlfriends I'd had, but there was something uniquely different about her, I couldn't quite put my finger on what it was. I had this weird feeling, a sense of wanting to protect her and wanting her to love this land as much as I did. I never had that with the others; it was just pure and unadulterated attraction with them, which usually wore off in time.

'What a beautiful day,' she said, whilst drinking in the spectacular scenery around her. She turned to face me and said, 'It makes you glad to be alive when we get days like this, a chance to melt away the mundane things in our lives and escape routine to just reflect on life and nature all around us.'

She brought out the best in me, something the others didn't. I don't really know why, maybe it's just plain and simply falling in love at long last. I knew I wanted to take her with me and show her the beauty of the land I loved.

Looking up at the cloudless, heliotrope-tinted sky, I said, 'Isn't it great to feel that warm sun on your skin?'

She replied, 'Yes I know exactly what you mean; days like this in early summer are few and far between.' There was silence between us for about three minutes, and we just drank in the potent atmosphere.

A strong sensation came over me that my past story was somehow intimately bound up with this remote place; its wild sacred beauty, sometimes violent, now romantic, uplifting, overwhelmed my very being. It felt like I was going back in time to the origins of life and time itself.

Gail had recently moved to Caithness from Glasgow where she had set up her own business working remotely as a finance consultant for clients all over the UK. She'd done her degree in Reykjavik University, then moved back to Scotland. She left her well-paid job in Glasgow to be nearer to her parents who had relocated to Caithness for the peace and quiet, as her father was slowly recovering from a major stroke.

We strolled along the narrow peat path, tiptoeing in single file to avoid sinking in the bog, whilst at the same time admiring the sheer openness and grandeur of the landscape all around us.

'Look over there.' Gail pointed to where a herd of deer were grazing a couple of hundred feet away. The deer had either an acute sense of hearing or smell, as they immediately turned and looked at us as if to say, clear off.

'Wow, what magnificent beasts, look at the antlers on that stag,' said Gail. The deer stopped grazing but kept staring at us. I almost read his thoughts. This was their domain, what the hell were we doing here interrupting their nice day? I grasped her hand, already realising that she was my soul mate.

Further along the path, we reached a natural viewpoint on the top of a crag overlooking the vista of Loch Eriboll on the extreme North West coast of mainland Scotland. We sat down together on a huge, rounded, striated boulder, our knees hunched into our chests.

'Where would this boulder have come from?' she asked. 'I've seen nothing like it in all the miles on our climb.'

'The rock boulder was a glacial erratic,' I explained, 'left stranded in time and place after the ice melted at the end of the last ice age thirteen thousand years ago. The rock we are sitting on is Lewisian Gneiss and this rock is the oldest rock type in

Europe, formed two and a half billion years ago along with the primaeval rocks of Greenland and Labrador.'

'Wow, you just can't get your head round two and a half billion years when compared with our short lifespan,' she replied.

Pointing to the west, I said, 'When the Atlantic Ocean opened up, this bit of West Sutherland and the Western Isles were left behind, stranded on the wrong side of the Atlantic, eventually joining with much younger continental pieces of Eurasia that would eventually become Scotland.'

Gail laughed in response. 'How the hell do you know all this?'

'Well,' I stated humbly, hoping I wasn't boring her, 'I studied Geology at university down in Leeds for a couple of years before I decided to ditch it for a real job, earning good money and all that.'

Gail replied, 'You never told me you were at university .'

'You never asked, My parents were really pissed off with me at the time, quite rightly so I guess,' I replied.

'Do you have more secrets in your past, John?'

'No, Gail, I don't, it's just that I don't want to bore you by giving you a blow-by-blow account of my life so far.'

Gail shrugged her shoulders and a silence descended on us as we scanned the vista before us, looking down the fifteen-hundred feet drop to Eriboll farm, the only habitation for many miles around and an old, red, telephone box, looking the worse for wear.

'Listen, do you hear a cuckoo in the distance?' I asked.

'It must be far away, but with no wind, you can hear as well as see for miles in the distance.'

We both now re-tuned our ears as if in a competition to hear the most delicate of nature's sounds.

After about a minute Gail exclaimed, 'You can just hear that waterfall faintly over the other side of the loch.'

'Our ears are adjusting to the silence and heightening our response.' I turned and smiled at her; thinking how compatible we were.

'Look, John.' She pointed to the Reay Forest mountain range. 'The summits of the mountains still have snow in the valleys.'

'That's the residual winter snow and it will be melted before the start of July.'

'The snow on the mountains is so perfect with the light-coloured scree slopes, it's stunning and rugged. I love it all.'

'I remember a few years ago when I walked the narrow ridge between the peaks of Foinaven at the June solstice. It was a fantastic experience. I spent the night on the summit near the trig point with brandy for company. Up there at three thousand feet, the sun did not set at midnight, it hovered and skirted the horizon between midnight and one am. A beautiful twilight and the range of colours; blue, orange, yellow and silver were breath-taking all over the clear northern sky.'

I scanned my mind and consciousness rapidly for the buried images of that day. The view from the top was amazing; I could make out the hills of Lewis, far away Birsay Island on Orkney and, looking over to where we are now sitting, the great rounded dome of Ben Hope, looming menacingly in the distance, with Loch Eriboll in the foreground. Pointing to Foinaven, I said, 'Look Gail, over there, that's where I was. Here, have a look through the binoculars, you should make out the trig point and cairn.' I handed her the binoculars hoping to illustrate my recollection of that day in time and space.

'I can make out a couple of climbers near the top; I don't think I could climb Foinaven, I don't have the confidence or the stamina to do that, but I'm definitely enjoying this trip. We have done about seven miles and cannot be higher than about fifteen hundred feet up.'

I put my arm around her waist.

She sighed and said, 'When you are in the wilderness like this, well away from the single-track road, you are in a totally different world.'

Little did I know at that time, these words she uttered would come back and haunt us.

Gail continued scanning the landscape in front of her through the binoculars and hollered out, 'John, look over there on the other side of the Loch, that wooden building on stilts, it looks odd.'

'Have you heard of Lotte Glob?' I asked.

'Yes,' she said. 'She's that ceramic artist from Durness. I've seen her work at the Balnakeil craft place at Durness.'

'Yes' I replied. 'Over the years she has been placing her artwork in some of the remote parts of North West Sutherland. I came upon one of her pieces of art hidden away in a remote gully on Foinaven near that whale fin peak over there on the ridge.' I pointed over to the ridge to show the rough location.

'What? She puts her art in the mountains around here?'

'Yep she does, the one I came across on Foinaven was tucked into a rock crevice, it looked like a vivid blue alien from another planet. It stood up to the arctic winter climate on the mountain. I have the picture of it on my iPhone.' I got my phone out and showed her the picture of the ceramic pottery in its lofty location. 'What you saw was her wooden house and studio on stilts on the other side of the loch.'

'That's a really remote place to live, away from it all, maybe great in summer but I would not fancy it in the winter,' she said.

'Did you not find it cold in Reykjavik in the winter?'

'Yes it was, but it was a great experience, I do love the northern landscapes, it's so special to me. It was in many ways an easy decision for me to move up from Glasgow; the call of the north was strong.'

We continued walking in silence for a few more minutes, then I suddenly felt queasy; the air seemed to shimmer and spark with static in front of us, something akin to a mirage on a hot day.

Gail felt the same thing. We looked at each other with expressions of disbelief. The shimmering intensified to the point where Gail and the surroundings broke up. The last thing I heard was her scream. I turned to grab onto her when the shimmering turned to total blackness and she was gone. My heart pounded at this impossible situation and her scream was the last sound I heard as it slowly attenuated to nothing.

I was in blackness, no Gail, no awareness of my body. Was I dead? The thought scared me. Did I take a stroke or a massive heart attack? I felt no pain, I felt nothing, and I was barely conscious.

Just as quickly as it went totally dark, the shimmering and static noise started up again, making me aware once again of sound and the sight of a shimmering Gail next to me. Everything around me spun, melding into splashes of vibrant colour, spinning out of control.

I asked myself, was this how life on this earth ends in a kaleidoscope of spinning colours? At that point, the spinning slowed down and the shimmering detail and resolution of reality slowly came back into view.

We both fell out of the shimmering veil at the same time. We ended up on all fours physically sick and vomiting.

Gail spoke first. 'What the hell was that? .'

'God only knows.'

We helped each other up, dusted ourselves down and took some water out of my rucksack. 'I think I need something stronger than water after this, I thought I was dying,' I said.

We looked nervously at each other, as neither of us could explain what had just happened.

As we drank the much-needed water, we looked about ourselves and had that feeling that something was not quite right. The view was much the same but the grass and heather were different. As we were acclimatising ourselves after the experience, we noticed the temperature was a lot higher than it was before the shimmering. The sheep track we were walking along had gone. On the west side of Loch Eriboll the houses that line the crofting township of Laid were gone, there was no visible sign of the road to Durness round the loch. We looked at each other in disbelief, scared to admit that we were somewhere different, yet similar to where we were before the *shimmering* event.

There was no tombolo at the head of Loch Eriboll. There was now a small island, the spit of land gone. No Limestone works and buildings, all gone. No Eriboll farm, road or telephone box. Instead, there was something inexplicable. About half a mile to the coast from where Eriboll farm should have been, there was what looked like a small medieval settlement, four longhouses set around crudely tilled land with smoke emanating from two of the longhouses.

We both came to the realisation that we had crossed some portal or Rubicon into a different world and time period.

Gail, now in tears, said, 'How can we get back? '

We watched with horror as Viking longboats turned around Whiten Head at the mouth of Loch Eriboll, heading for what looked like a rudimentary wooden pier at what was Portnacon.

We looked at each other in disbelief as we realised we were back around 1000 AD, at the height of the Viking settlement of northern Scotland. As we watched we noticed a beacon being lit at Portnacon, as if to welcome the boats back home.

I pointed to the sun above Foinaven. 'Not only have we gone back in date, but the sun is also a lot lower than it was before that shimmering.'

I looked at my watch which showed 6:30 p.m, we had added three hours but gone back a thousand years. Our basic need for shelter and food for the night was fast approaching.

Gail was in shock.

'We have to survive somehow, but first, we should try walking back to where we think the shimmering started and walk through it again,' I said.

We held hands to comfort each other and retraced our steps on a path that was no longer there. After a few attempts going forward and back; nothing.

'We have to get down from the hill and into the shelter of the valley. Luckily it's early summer, so we won't freeze at night,' I said.

'If you think so, but what about the people in these long houses, they may see us. God only knows if they will help us.'

I thought that we might need their help for food and shelter, but how they would react to two very odd strangers was another story. It was then I thought to try my mobile phone but, as I expected, we were on our own one thousand years in the past with no assistance available from the 21st century.

It was at that point that I became aware of two men making their way up the heather slope towards us, shouting something like '*hverr eru phu.*'

Panic set in, we had been spotted.

'Don't run, that will make things worse, let's just try and convince them we mean no harm,' I said. The men slowed down. They looked like medieval characters, but had axes in their hands. I instinctively put my hands up to show I had no weapons. The older of the two repeated his words, '*hverr eru phu.*'

Adrenalin rushed as I held my ear with one hand and waved the other to indicate I didn't understand.

Gail recognised they were speaking a version of Old Norse and understood *eru phu* as 'who are you?'

She told me to let her speak, as she knew some Icelandic from her university days in Reykjavik. Icelandic is very close to the Old Norse language. She pointed to me and back to her and said, '*Fra Katanes.*'

I recognised the Old Norse name for Caithness. The men looked at each other and seemed to understand. They shook their heads in agreement. Then Gail pointed eastwards and said '*Auster,*' the eastern lands.

The older man pointed to the younger man and said '*Brither Loki* 'which even I recognised from our Caithness dialect as meaning brother. Gail pointed to me and said, '*Gitfur* 'which she explained meant *we are married,* as that best fits for these times.

They laughed at that and came closer to us.

'Wow 'I said, 'that could have been very nasty.'

Gail replied, 'Looks like they are friendly, thank God.'

Then they pointed down to Loch Eriboll and said, '*Heim Eryabol Borg.*'

Gail translated it as their home.

They then spoke to each other in words Gail did not recognise, but they pushed us and indicated the farm below where I assumed our destination would be.

Gail took out a bottle of water to take a sip. The men wanted to see this weird, clear container. Gail said,'*Vatn* 'which they recognised as water and offered them a drink, which they took and said, '*takk fyrir*' which Gail translated to me as thanks.

The sun had now set over the summit of Foinaven in the distance and I checked my watch, it was 8:30 p.m. and still plenty of light. As we descended the hill and got closer to the buildings, we heard the sounds of cattle and children. Smoke rose vertically from the thatched longhouses. We noted the land was cultivated very differently; there was lots of low grass on the east side of the loch and good farmland with very little heather except on the upland areas. The warmth in the air was noticeable. The temperature felt like the high twenties, more like France than the north of Scotland. The climate was obviously a lot warmer in the 11th century than in the 21st. I noticed they were growing a form of wheat and barley in the long strip fields adjacent to the hamlet.

We arrived at the longhouses, barns and huts. There was a pungent odour of animals and people living in close quarters. The children ran up to us in awe of what to them must have been a very strange sight and touched our *weird* clothing. Older people were more reticent and held back, talking among themselves in low tones whilst at the same time giving us the once over.

The two men with us addressed their people and, pointing to us said, '*Their eru ókunnugir frá Kataness og eru týnd fjall.*'

I looked at Gail in the hope she could translate.

'It sounds roughly like they think we are strangers from Caithness and were lost in the mountains,' she said.

One of the men pointed to me and said, '*tala.*'

Gail said, 'They want you to speak. You better say something.'

I pointed to myself and said, ' John.'

I pointed to Gail and she said, '*eg er Gail.*'

They looked at each other, '*Eg Arni ,brither Loki,*' said one.

Gail translated it to Arni and his brother Loki.

The men pointed to the other side of Loch Erribol where the longships were now berthed and said, '*Norethmenn eru komnir, ertu ath fara aftur meth theim.*'

Gail asked them to repeat what they said and then picked up on the meaning. 'They say the Norse have arrived from the home country, and they think we are heading to Norway on the boat's return trip but got lost on the hills.

We agreed. '*Ja*'

'*Matur*,' said Gale and made a gesture of eating. They took us into the communal long house where some porridge concoction was cooking slowly on an iron stove in the centre of the floor.

They seated us in the position at the table as if we were honoured guests and we looked around. It was comfortable and not too hot given the very warm temperature outside. It was like being in a living museum. The longhouse was about thirty feet wide and one hundred feet long. There were two rows of wooden columns that ran the length of the house supporting the high points of the roof, which was thatched. The wall was a mixture of wooden planks and wattle and daub. The longhouse was shaped like an upturned boat.

The smoke from the central fires escaped through the gaps in the thatching and the roof vents that were opened to let smoke escape and to let in light. With no windows, it must be a gloomy existence in winter with only fires and oil lamps for a meagre light.

The Longhouse had three doors on three sides so that depending on the direction of the wind, any door could be used. There were what looked like box beds that they called *kistas* all down one side of the longhouse, presumably where they slept in family groups. The space was busy and noisy as they all lived communally, with the animals living at the far end of the longhouse.

Finding peace and some privacy in here would be impossible, as they all cooked, ate, worked, slept, and made love in close quarters.

In one corner was a vertical sort of loom, with spindle, whorls and weights, which I assumed they used to make the cloth hangings which gave a small modicum of privacy.

In the hubbub of meal preparation, a young woman came over and said, '*mjoreth*,' a word which Gail did not recognize. We were offered some liquid in a horn, it tasted like some form of beer made from oats or barley. I drunk it heartily as our water bottle was now empty. Gail did the same, thinking that a refusal would offend them.

To the left of us a young man was fashioning a comb out of bone whilst singing a repetitive verse in a lilting Norse tone. Our main course was a stodgy porridge, which tasted bland, but we were so hungry, we ate it anyway.

'*Takk fyrir,*' said Gail. Thank you.

It was a that point, another Norsemen arrived. After exchanging pleasantries with a few people, he looked at us and glowered. Even without knowing old Norse, it was obvious he was asking who we were and why were we there.

'Vatn Erjabol, knorr, hofn, Northur Auster Vegr.'

They are planning to take us across loch Erriboll to join the Viking longboat in the harbour and north-east to Norway,' whispered Gail.

Stunned, I grabbed her hand.

The Norseman came over to us, looked us up and down and said, '*Koma.*'

We instinctively knew to go with him and we followed him out of the longhouse to the shore. A small boat awaited to take us across the loch to the wooden harbour where Portnacon would be one thousand years later. He gestured to us to get into the boat and blasted what seemed like instructions to the oarsman. The crossing took about forty minutes. by now it was near 10 p.m. and the light was slowly fading into dusk.

When we stepped off the small boat, we noticed another eight young men and women already standing on the wooden pier, guarded, it seemed, by a couple of Norseman. We became very suspicious of our fate. Along with them, we were herded into a hut. It was at that point, that my mobile phone fell out of my pocket and was immediately noticed by a Norseman. He picked it up and must have pressed the *on* button as the phone lit up. In shock, he dropped it and smashed it with his axe. He looked up and shouted, '*anskoti*' which Gail translated as being the devil.

The other eight people in the hut looked at us, with guarded suspicion.

Gail made some basic conversation with them and they seemed to be in agreement.

A young man who looked as if he may be a farm hand pointed at us and said, '*Thralls.*'

Gail looked at me in horror and said, '*We are slaves, they are taking us to Norway as slaves.*' I put my head down in disbelief as if things could not get any worse.

There was loud shouting and drinking going on near the adjacent longboat and the next thing we knew, our guard, joined by the other three Norsemen, manhandled the ten of us into the cordoned-off section of the longboat.

As we sat huddled together, I wondered just how much worse was this going to get.

'Helvetis skitevar,' a Norseman shouted.

'What is he saying?' I whispered.

She looked scared. 'You really don't want to know.'

The only member of the crew left to guard us came over to Gail, grabbed her wrist and said, '*Eg aelta ath fokka.*'

Gail screamed, obviously knowing the gist of what he said. The Norsemen laughed and one of them went away leaving Gail to the mercy of the remaining man.

I tried to stop him touching her and he pushed me back with a force that almost dislocated my shoulder. It became clear that with his strength there was no need for two guards.

Gail screamed, 'John, help me.'

I made a supreme effort to stop him, but again the Norseman shouted at me and punched me with such force that I fell back, incapacitated.

Just then the other slaves rose up and leapt on the Norseman, releasing Gail from his grip. Gail kicked the man between the legs with such force, he stumbled and fell over. It was then two slaves set upon him and knocked him out cold.

They saw their chance and ran from the longship and into the freedom of the northern twilight.

Other crew members, hearing the commotion, noticed the slaves fleeing and started chasing them with axes in hand. There was a piercing scream and a female tumbled to the ground with an axe in her back. Another two Norsemen jumped on the longship to stop us from following them and noticed their crew member out for the count, which seemed to ignite their temper.

The slaves were captured and returned to the longboat. They were viciously beaten as punishment. The Norsemen regarded us with malice. It looked like we were going to get a good beating as well.

It was then the Norseman lying on the deck came back to consciousness. He got up and started kicking one of the boys in the stomach. We waited anxiously for our turn. I looked at Gail and she me, and I thought, *it's over, this is it, we are finished.* My life flashed before me in seconds. Past, present and future all happened at once, in different dimensions.

We had somehow crossed into another dimension running parallel to our 21st-century version. As I tried to make sense of this, the longboat crew headed for us.

It was then, out of the blue, came the shimmering we experienced a good eight hours ago. The spinning kaleidoscope of moving colours broke up my vision.

Gail grabbed my hand. 'It's happening again, can you see it, John?'

'Yes,' I was able to whisper.

My last words before the shimmering colours faded to black were, 'When or where on earth will we end up now?'

Saving the Seals

by Catherine M Byrne

Eric watched his brother, Olaf, make eye contact with yet another young girl. Every time the ferry brought a new group, Olaf was right there, planning his next conquest. With his rugged good looks and the charm of the devil, he left a string of broken hearts behind him.

'I wish you wouldn't,' muttered Eric, as the passengers disembarked.

'Why? I make them no promises.' White teeth flashed in a darkly tanned face, deep brown eyes glinting with mischief. 'I leave them with happy memories.'

'You hurt them; you know you do.'

'How did I ever come to have such a self-righteous brother? How old are you now – fifteen already. Never mind, your turn will come.' He tousled the younger boy's hair and Eric pulled away, irritated

Secretly, Eric both admired and envied his brother's charm. Everything Olaf did was performed with deft flamboyance and almost sensual movements. Even the way he threw creels together was guaranteed to attract a knot of spectators. Visitors to the little fishing port would watch him with 'oohs,' and 'ahhs,' and 'How did you do that?' And Olaf would answer with grins and winks and compliments. He would tell them legends of the islands to the background music of seabirds and waves racing up the beach, rattling the shingle and slapping against the pier wall. The salt of the sea scented the wind. Painted cottages along the harbourfront provided a backdrop. by the time he had finished his tales, it seemed to Eric, Olaf could have his pick of any woman there.

But there was something different about the girl who arrived that morning in the early spring. She was small and slim with a quick easy smile and masses of red flowing hair. The brothers noticed her immediately, as much for herself as for the poster she held above her head. The poster depicting the bloody body of a baby seal.

'Not again! Not another bunch of crusaders with a so-called argument against the seal culling,' said Dan, an old fisherman who was passing on his skills to the boys. 'Let them try to make a living at the fishing and they'd soon sing a different song.'

'I'll see to her.' With an amused grin, Olaf strode along the jetty. 'Would it interest you to know that that poster is many decades out of date?' he asked, leaning against the parapet.

The girl turned towards him, hair flying around her head, hazel eyes flecked with fire. Eric thought she was the most magnificent thing he had ever seen.

'I doubt if anything you said would interest me,' she said.

'The cull is controlled and the seals are shot—no more clubbing to death,' said Olaf.

'Why do they have to be killed at all?'

'They destroy the fish. There is no longer enough fishing for seals and humans. Which species would you rather cull?'

Her cheeks turned pink and her voice rose. 'There are plenty of alternatives for humans. There are none for seals.'

'Why do you care?' Olaf pushed himself from the wall and walked slowly towards her, his smile indolent.

'I care about the environment as a whole. There are more fish destroyed by pollution and careless trawling than by seals.' Her head was thrown back, her chin jutting out, her stance defiant.

'Why don't I walk you to your lodgings? Who knows, you might convert me yet.' He reached down and picked up her bag.

'Let me tell you this…' the girl started.

Eric didn't listen to the rest of the sentence. He had seen the light in his brother's eye and the answering spark in the girl's. And he knew the game had begun.

Much later, when Olaf introduced them, she grasped Eric's hand firmly. Her cheeks were flushed, her manner, mollified.

'So you're Olaf's little brother.'

He baulked at the word little. He didn't understand why his heart beat faster and the words thickened and stuck in his throat. This range of new emotions both scared and thrilled him. Though he knew she hardly noticed him at all, he felt the instant need to be near her.

Olaf had changed too. He didn't appear so confident when she was around and he watched her with a lost look in his eyes that Eric had never seen before.

She continued to talk animatedly about the environment and how man was destroying the planet and she begged the brothers to join her in the march against the culling of the seals.

Eric was enthralled. In him, she found a willing convert. Olaf, however, declined.

'I'm a fisherman,' he explained. 'And it's the fishermen who wanted the seals culled in the first place – remember?'

'But I'm not a fisherman, so what's to stop me going?' said Eric.

'Then go for it, little brother. Though I doubt the protests will do any good.'

Eric spent a blissful few weeks in the company of Tara Lamont and her friends. But in the evenings, she and Eric joined Olaf on the beach where the moon cast its shimmering pebbles across the ocean. They cooked fish over an open fire and talked of the day's events. Then they would lie back on a rug and look at the stars and listen to the sounds of the ocean; the soft swish of waves on the sand; the unearthly cries of the seals as if they yearned for something that could never be theirs; the cry of a solitary gull as it flew home to roost.

Eric dreaded that hour because he knew that Tara and his brother were waiting for him to depart. And he would go home, dragging his feet, not daring to look back. The unfamiliar pain in his heart was already too great.

Sleep evaded Eric on these hot summer nights as he lay with his mind in a tangle and waited for his brother's return. Often his parents would already have started their day before he heard Olaf's soft whistle and his mother's reprimands. But soon there would be laughter, for Olaf would reassure his parents and they would forgive him, as they forgave him everything.

'Where do you live?' asked Tara one night. Eric waited, mentally rolling his eyes, imagining Olaf bringing her home and introducing her to his parents.

'You can't see our house from here,' Olaf said.

'At the other side then. I'd like to go there.'

'Now why on earth would you want to do that?' Olaf pulled her to the ground where they tumbled about shrieking with glee. No longer able to stand seeing them together, Eric ran down the beach and into the sea, allowing the water to caress his hot skin, run through his hair and over his body like loving fingers. He was a strong swimmer and each stroke took him farther out into the bay, until, exhausted, he turned back towards the shore.

'You little fool,' Olaf shouted as Eric shook himself free of the water. 'What do you think you're doing?' He grabbed his young brother by the shoulder and for a moment looked as if he might hit him.

'I only went for a swim,' replied the boy, jerking away. 'I didn't think you'd notice I'd gone.'

Olaf sighed, his hands falling to his side. 'Don't ever do that to me again.'

'Oh, come on you two. He's back now.' Tara put an arm around Eric's shoulder. 'Your brother was worried. He thought you might have drowned.'

Eric shrugged her arm off, at the same time wanting it to stay where it was. 'I'm sure he was worried about *something*.' He stormed up the beach with a look of fire in his brother's direction.

Olaf did not stay out late that night. When he returned home he sat on Eric's bed.

'What's wrong, little brother?' he said.

'You know what's wrong,' Eric replied, keeping his back turned. 'You're just leading her on – like all the rest.'

Olaf was silent for a minute. 'You like her, don't you?' he said at last. 'Well, I like her too. Maybe I'll ask her to stay.'

Eric shot round, anger coursing through him like a fire. 'You can't do that! What about our plans?'

'We'll have to change things a little, that's all.'

'But you can't.' Eric turned away, embarrassing tears welling up in his eyes.

The weather was cooler the following day and grey clouds rolled in from the east. The bog cotton danced in the fields and the sea was a flat, grey blanket speckled with flecks of white. Olaf's face was set, his eyes, dark circled. The brothers worked together in silence, tightening the nets around the creel frames.

Suddenly she was there, coming towards them, the wind blowing her hair away from her face and plastering her long skirt around the shape of her legs. She laughed as she drew alongside Olaf, her face turned up for his kiss.

'I wish I didn't have to go back.' She wrapped her arms around his waist. 'I've decided I hate the traffic and the smog.'

'Maybe you won't have to.' Olaf returned her hug.

Anger bubbled in Eric. 'I'm off.' His voice was barely more than a murmur.

'What's wrong?' Tara looked surprised. Olaf whispered something to her and she giggled.

Eric turned and ran, embarrassment lending speed to his feet. They were laughing at him! Making fun of his feelings – how could they? He never wanted to see either of them again.

Olaf found him on the beach the following morning skimming pebbles across the water. Without speaking, he picked up a handful of stones of his own. Eric stopped and sat down. What was the point, his brother was better than him at skimming anyway.

'She's meant to go today,' said Olaf, without turning around.

'I did listen to what you said. I did try to end it last night.'

Eric lifted his head. 'What did she say?'

'She was hurt, very hurt. I've been up all night wrestling with this. I'm going to ask her to stay. We'll make it work, Eric. Be happy for me.'

'But you can't.'

'I can do anything I chose.' He picked up another pebble and hurled it angrily across the water. It bounced four times before it sank.

Somewhere in the distance, a rocket shot skyward.

'Olaf, Olaf,' Old Dan appeared over the rise. 'Come on. There's an oil tankard in trouble on the north side. We're a man short on the lifeboat and you're the best we've got.'

Olaf glanced at his watch. 'Eric,' he bent down and looked into his brother's face. 'Go see Tara. Tell her what's happened and tell her not to go until we've talked. Tell her to wait for the next ferry. I have to see her. Can I trust you to do that?'

Eric looked into the anxious eyes of his brother and nodded, but in the pockets of his dungarees, he crossed his fingers

She found Eric mending nets among the boulders behind the quay. 'I've been looking for you,' she said, lowering herself beside him.

'Why?' He kept his head averted.

'Weren't you even going to say goodbye? Is it something I've done? And where is Olaf?'

He raised his head to look at her and his heart melted. Her eyes were red and puffed as if she had been crying all night.

'Oh, Eric, I thought he loved me, I really did.'

He wanted to put his arm around her but lacked the confidence. If only he were older.

'I've made such a fool of myself,' she said.

'How?'

'I told him how I felt. I thought it was the same for him. How could I be so wrong?'

She buried her head in her hands and leaned against Eric. He tensed, unsure of what to say or how to act. All he knew was that somehow he wanted to ease her hurt.

'He does care for you – it's just that he can't be with you. It's not possible.'

'Why – is he married?' Tara bolted upright.

'No, nothing like that. Go back to the city and forget about us.'

'I can't, it's too late. Why is it not possible? I have to know.'

Eric stared at the middle distance, wishing he had never started this. 'I only said that to make you feel better.' He longed for the beach to open and swallow him up.

'I don't believe you. Tell me why.'

He stood up and dusted the sand from his clothes. 'He's going into the priesthood.' He blurted out at last. 'He took a year off to make sure it's what he wanted.'

Tara stared at him. 'Olaf—a priest?' Then her eyes lit up. 'But if he took a year off, then he isn't sure.'

'He is sure. He told me to tell you goodbye. He couldn't face doing it himself. He cares too much.' The words did not come easily. Eric was unused to lying but was spurred on by the belief that what he did was for the best. 'He's made up his mind,' he added vehemently.

'And you found it hard to tell me? You're such a kind boy. I'll never forget you—neither of you. Even if Olaf isn't man enough to face me himself.' Tears ran unchecked down her cheeks. Eric fought to keep his own lip from trembling as he swallowed the lump in his throat.

'The ferry is about to leave. Come and wave me goodbye.'

Eric shook his head, avoiding her gaze. 'I'd rather stay here.'

She kissed his cheek and he felt the sensation of it long after she was gone. He watched her walk to the pier, his heart in pieces.

The ferry pushed from the land. Eric heard a shout as Olaf came running down the hill.

'Where is she? Didn't you tell her to wait?'

'No.'

'I don't understand…Eric?'

'I…I told her you were going into the priesthood.'

'What? Why on earth would you say that?'

'Would you rather I told her the truth? It's for her own good. You know I'm right.'

'You can't live my life for me – not you – not our parents. I'm going after her.' There was a desperation in his voice that scared Eric. The calm confidence that was so much part of his brother had gone.

'How? All the boats have been taken round the north side, remember.'

'Then there's only one thing I can do.' Olaf began to peel off his clothes.

'If you try to swim out there then…' Eric's voice trailed to a halt as his brother made a perfect dive into the churning firth.

'Then I'm coming with you.' He kicked off his own garments and followed with strong, well-defined strokes.

'Go back, you fool,' cried Olaf, but it was already too late. The cold current of the rip tide had him in its grip.

Eric felt his body convulse in a spasm and he sank to the bottom like a stone. Minutes later he resurfaced, a stronger and faster swimmer. Still shuddering after the shock of metamorphosis, he looked at his brother, twisting with an almost forgotten ease in the water. He, too, had lost his mortality in an effort to reach his love.

From the deck of the ferry, Tara noticed them briefly but paid little attention. After all, why would she be interested in a couple of black-eyed seals when her heart was breaking?

A Different Ball Game

by Margaret Wood

'Get the ball. Get the ball.' Adam yelled at the figures racing across his television screen and reached for a can of lager. He tugged the ring pull. The beer fizzed into life.

'Oi. Watch what you're doing. You nearly drowned me.'

The voice came from around his knee and, looking down, he saw a small figure about eighteen inches high. It was wiping froth from its face with the sleeve of a shapeless, black garment. It had deathly pale cheeks and, with its explosion of dark hair and white painted lips, it resembled a miniature Goth. A pair of wings sprouted from its back.

Too much beer thought Adam. But it was only his second can. Too much telly then. He rubbed his eyes and looked again. It was still there, gazing up at him. Correction. Smirking up at him. He'd seen that look often enough on Chloe's face to know that his visitor must be female.

'You're not seeing things,' she said. 'I'm your Fairy Godmother and I've come to tell you that you *shall* go to the ball.'

'What ball?' said Adam. 'I'm not going to any ball.'

'But I heard you. You were shouting about getting to the ball.'

'Oh, that ball. That was a football.'

'No dancing then?'

Adam considered the clumsy footwork that Rovers had been displaying.

'Definitely no dancing.'

The fairy looked worried. 'HQ's not going to be pleased with me. All these years waiting for you to ask for something and it turns out to be a mistake.'

'You mean you've been my ...' Adam paused, embarrassed at what he was about to say,

'Fairy Godmother? Yeah. Ever since you were baptised Adam Horatio Nelson Henderson.'

'How did you know that?' For most of his twenty-five years, Adam had been happy to forget his mother's moment of madness at the font.

The fairy grinned. 'Been there. Saw it. Ate the christening cake.'

'You don't look old enough.'

'Nuh. We never do. Unless we choose to. Remember that old woman you helped with her shopping yesterday? That was me.'

'No it wasn't. It was Mrs Thomas from upstairs.'

The fairy looked sheepish. 'Yeah. So it was. But it could have been me. I can be anybody I like. Actually, I was there checking up on you. You've turned out not too badly, Adam Horatio Nelson Henderson. More than can be said for that misery-guts female who was with you.' Her voice changed. 'She's only got a couple of bags, Adam. She'll easily manage. We're already late for the film.'

It was a wickedly accurate impersonation of Chloe and Adam burst out laughing. 'She's not your type,' said the fairy. 'Why don't I run a few ideas past you and we'll soon find the girl of your dreams?'

A movement on the TV screen caught Adam's eye. 'Not just now we won't. The second half's starting.'

The fairy leapt onto the arm of his chair. 'Great,' she said. 'You can explain all about it. What's this off-side thing?'

Adam's heart sank. He'd been here before. His night would be ruined. But at the end of forty-five minutes plus extra time, it was as though the fairy and he had been watching matches together forever.

'Well, F.G.,' he said, tossing aside an empty can. 'We woz robbed.'

'Defniate... definy... sure thing.' The fairy held out her empty egg cup. 'Any more of that fizzy stuff?'

Before Adam could reply, there was a long ring on the doorbell. He heaved himself out of his chair. The bell rang again.

'Impatient,' said the fairy.

Somehow Adam was not surprised to find Chloe on the doorstep.

'I thought we had a date,' she said.

Adam had a vague memory of suggesting a drink after the match, but what with the fairy and extra time it had gone clean out of his head. There was a sound behind him and he saw Chloe's eyes widen.

'Football match, eh?' she said.

Adam spun around. The fairy was lounging in the doorway. It had to be the fairy. Who else could it be? But the tiny Goth was gone. In her place was an attractive young woman swathed only in his dressing gown. She had a tousle of auburn hair and cat-like eyes. It was clear she had recently enjoyed the cream.

'Time for the recorded highlights,' she purred.

When Chloe had gone, leaving only her perfume on the air and the imprint of her hand on Adam's cheek, he turned on the fairy.

'She's not right for you,' she defended herself. 'I know the very person. She'll be perfect.'

'I'm not interested.'

'Huh,' said the fairy. 'You will be.'

Next morning, if it wasn't for Chloe's abusive message on his answer phone, Adam would have been convinced that he had dreamed the whole episode. As it was, by the time he arrived at work, he had filed it away as an amusing story for some future dinner party. That was until he met Lucy, the new girl in accounts, and found himself face-to-face with the redhead of the night before. It was obvious now what F.G. had been up to. This must be the girl she had in mind for him.

That night, the fairy was waiting for him in his flat. The television was switched to the sports channel. Anger bubbled inside him. What cheek? Marching into his life. Interfering.

'So how did it go?' Her cheeks shone pink with excitement through the white makeup. She was like an eager child and his anger melted.

'She's a lovely lady,' he said.

'And?'

'And clever. Too clever. *Financial Times* type clever.'

'Oh.' Her face fell but brightened almost immediately. 'So next time, easy on the intelligence?'

'There won't be a next time,'

'Oh look,' she said 'The match is starting.'

Over the following weeks, Adam met:-

Carly ('Brexit? That's a cereal, isn't it?')

Eloise (voice like a diesel engine)

Rosa (opera singer in the Pavarotti mould)

Lindsay ('A lettuce leaf's enough for me' – which wouldn't have been so bad if said lettuce leaf hadn't cost Adam thirty-six pounds in the *Café Rouge.*)

The time had come to tell FG that enough was enough.

He had expected her to be installed in front of the television on his return, but his flat was in darkness and strangely empty. He hadn't realised how much he enjoyed having someone there to welcome him. Perhaps it *was* time to consider a serious relationship. But he would do it his own way. He closed his eyes and, praying that no one would ever find out about it, he called out, 'I wish I could go to the ball.'

Within seconds he heard the whirring of wings and a female figure materialised beside him. She was as large as an opera singer, Rosa, and dressed in totally unsuitable gauzy garments.

'Well, Mr Henderson,' she boomed. 'We meet at last. We have heard so much about you.'

'You're not my Fairy Godmother.'

'Indeed, no. Fortune was watching over me the day *you* were born. No, I'm afraid Serena has been taken off your case.'

Serena. He had never asked if she had a name. He thought of the feisty little creature he had come to know. Serena. It didn't suit her.

'Why?' he said.

'HQ feels she's not been trying hard enough. Any Fairy Godmother worth her wings would have had you done and dusted by now. However, that's beside the point. No doubt you will be pleased to hear that you *shall* go to the ball.'

'But I only said it … I don't really want ….' Adam's voice trailed away under the fairy's stern gaze.

'Mr Henderson, when I say you *shall* go to the ball, believe me you *shall*.' She fished into the bodice of her dress. 'In fact, I have the ticket here.'

Adam took the piece of card. 'The Lord Mayor's ball. But it's tonight. How can I possibly go tonight?' Adam thought of poor Serena being made to feel a failure. 'You've really messed up here, haven't you?' he said with satisfaction.

'Not at all,' said the fairy. 'Unless …' She looked worried. 'You can dance, can't you?'

Dancing lessons had been another of his mother's whims. 'Actually, I'm pretty nifty on my feet.'

'Splendid. Now stand still.' The fairy waved her wand. 'There. You *can* go to the ball.'

Adam found himself wearing an elegant evening suit with a scarlet cummerbund. In spite of himself, he was impressed.

'Now go,' said the fairy.

Adam hesitated. 'What? No pumpkin?'

'Oh, for Heaven's sake, take a taxi.'

'And will I meet the princess there?'

'Princess? What princess?'

'My partner. The love of my life. Home by midnight and all that.'

'Good gracious, I'd almost forgotten.' Another wave of the wand and standing beside Adam was a dainty figure in a sparkling evening gown. He only recognised her by her mischievous dark eyes. A warm feeling flowed over him.

'F.G.?' he said.

'Of course, it's most irregular,' said the large fairy. 'But there are precedents. Poor, dear Iolanthe. Now go, children, and be happy.' With that, she disappeared.

'Shall we?' said Adam and held his breath. So much depended on her answer.

'Yeah,' said F.G. reaching up to kiss him. 'I'll put the telly on. You get the beer.'

And Adam knew that they would live happily ever after.

Curse of the Caithness Quaich

by John Knowles

The candle on Fergus Mackay's workbench gutted violently as an icy draft crept through a gap between the window and frame of his Dunnet Bay workshop. He let out an involuntary yawn, as the old clock in the corner chimed for the twelfth time. He'd been working on the silver quaich all day, unusual for such a skilled silversmith. But this was no ordinary piece. This drinking vessel was to be a wedding gift from James Sinclair, twelfth Earl of Caithness to his new bride Jane. It had to be perfect. The Earl had requested the quaich be delivered to his home at Barrogill Castle in time for his wedding the following week.

December 1783 had been particularly cold, with unrelenting snowfall during the last few days of the year. Taking off his glasses, Fergus yawned again and rubbed his tired eyes. Brushing away his white, collar-length hair, he examined his finished masterpiece. The quaich sparkled and glistened in the candlelight. He allowed himself a brief, self-satisfying smile for a job done well. Within the next few days, he'd have to brave the inclement weather and deliver the quaich to Barrogill Castle, where the wedding was to take place, on the second day of the New Year.

Six months later, and after numerous reminders, not a penny piece had been received from the earl in payment for the quaich. Fergus became more and more embittered towards the earl. As summer turned to autumn, there was no doubt in his mind; Earl Sinclair had taken him for a fool. He thumped his workbench, causing a number of tools to fall on the floor.

'Curse the Quaich and all who possess it,' he muttered through gritted teeth. Having invested almost all of his capital in the silver to make the gift, the old man was almost ruined.

***

'Break in? You said nothing about breaking in.'

'Come on, just a quick look inside and then we'll head back.' Will Baxter shook his head and mounted his mountain bike. 'What's the matter, you scared or something? Come on, Will, we'll be fine, believe me. Who in the name of God is going to see us, out here in the middle of nowhere?'

Apart from the gamekeeper's cottage, Dalnawillan Lodge stood alone, miles from anywhere down a badly rutted track. During winter, it was often too icy to traverse. Westerdale was the nearest settlement which itself consisted of only a couple of houses. Battered over the years by the relentless Caithness weather, paint was peeling off the window and doorframes. A few roofing tiles lay smashed on the ground and the once brilliant white-rendered walls were now a shabby, light grey. The lodge had been built in a truly beautiful spot; with the River Thurso running to one side and wild open moor all around.

Adam McTaggart and William Baxter had been friends for years and had just finished their final year at Wick High School. They were making the most of their few weeks of freedom before seriously looking for jobs. Adam had always been a bad influence on his quieter friend, but somehow they'd managed to keep out of any serious trouble.

'Oh for pity's sake, let's just take a wee look inside and then I promise we'll go,' Adam said, but with a touch of aggression to his voice.

'But what if the gamekeeper sees us?' Will replied nervously.

'Oh, there's no need to worry about him. He'll be out somewhere on the estate.'

With a sigh, Will laid his bike on the ground. 'Okay, but just five minutes and then I'm gone, understand?'

'Yes, okay, whatever.'

The two boys walked around the lodge, looking for a way to get inside. Despite the state of the place, both were surprised that there were no broken windows or doors left ajar. Putting his shoulder to a door at the rear of the property, Adam gave it a shove. The rotten wood splintered and he stumbled into a darkened room.

Once accustomed to the dim light, he saw he was in a kitchen and activated the torch on his mobile phone. An old Belfast sink with bits of grit and dirt at the bottom, stood in front of a grimy window. An unwashed mug and plate sat on the wooden draining board, obviously abandoned decades ago. The room smelt musty, with mildew everywhere.

Adam ran a finger along a shelf which felt slimy and damp to the touch, an ancient gas cooker covered in burnt-on grease and grime stood against one wall, rusting pots and pans were scattered all over the work surfaces. Whoever had lived here either left in a hurry or had no concept of order or tidiness. Passing through an open door, the boys found themselves in a narrow corridor with doors off to each side.

Will wrung his hands nervously. 'I think we should get out of here before someone sees us,' he stammered.

Adam looked to the heavens with contemptuous eyes. 'You really are a wimp, aren't you? We've not explored the rest of the house yet. Who knows what we might find.'

The first door on the left creaked as he pushed it open. They found themselves in a huge room with a large bay window. Scraggy curtains hung limply from a rail that was coming away from the wall. A threadbare rug covered the centre of the floor, splintered floorboards showed around its edges.

'This floor looks like it's about to give way,' Will said.

Adams's eyes had been drawn towards the glass cabinet on the other side of the room. On the top shelf was a silver, two-handed drinking cup. 'Hey, look at that,' Adam said, excitement in his voice. 'If it's made of silver or platinum, it will be worth a small fortune.'

Will knew what was coming next.

'I'm having that,' Adam said, with a massive grin.

Will frowned, beads of perspiration beading his forehead. He should never have let Adam persuade him to come inside the lodge.

'Adam you can't. It doesn't belong to you. I'm getting out of here.'

Adam gave him a withering look. 'Oh, for God's sake, don't be such a wimp. I'm sure we'll be fine.' With that, Adam made his way across to the cabinet. The boards creaked and groaned beneath his feet, a few of them splintering under the weight. After forcing the cabinet's lock, he put his hand inside and pulled out the quaich. It felt freezing cold. Despite its tarnished condition, he was still able to read the words engraved on the side. It read,

'To celebrate the marriage of James Sinclair, twelve Earl of Caithness, to Jane Campbell on 2nd of January 1784.'

'Wow, take a look at this. It's nearly two hundred and forty years old! I bet it's worth a fortune.'

'I doubt it,' Will retorted. 'It'll be worthless. I mean why would someone leave something old and valuable behind?'

Adam gave Will a dirty look.

Will sometimes wondered how he'd become friends with someone who could be so hateful.

Adam slipped the quaich into his jacket pocket and carefully made his way to the door. Suddenly there was a splintering and cracking noise as one of the boards gave way. His foot went straight through and he fell back. He let out a deafening scream. 'Bloody hell, my ankle, I think I've broken my ankle.'

Will tiptoed warily across the floor to help his fallen comrade. 'You've probably just strained it. Now who's the wimp?' Will retorted with a grin.

The look of disdain on Adam's face was unmistakable. 'Okay, very funny I'm sure. Now will you bloody well give me a hand?'

Will carefully pulled at the floorboard, which broke with a crack. Gently he manoeuvred Adam's foot until he was able to free it. His face contorted in agony, he tried to stand up, but fell back. 'Oh my God, how the hell are we going to get home. I'll never be able to ride my bike like this.'

'Well, we can't stay here that's for sure,' Will said. 'I told you we shouldn't have come inside.'

'Okay, okay, I get the message, but that's not going to help us a whole lot just now, is it?' Blood seeped through his sock.

Will bit his lip. 'Look Adam, we're going to have to call for help, or we'll be stuck here forever.'

Adam gave him a withering look. 'Brilliant idea, Einstein, and let the cops know we've broken in and nicked some silver.'

'You mean *you've* nicked some silver, not *we*. I've got nothing to do with it,' Will snapped back. 'So what are we going to do, smart arse?'

He thought for a moment. 'If we can get you back outside, we can pretend you just fell off your bike and then call for an ambulance.'

'Worth a try I guess. Give them a call now and by the time they come, we'll be out of here.'

Will pulled his phone out of his pocket only for his heart to sink like a lead dandelion seed. No signal. Suddenly they were both shivering, goose bumps appearing on their arms. The temperature of the room had unexpectedly dropped.

Will's heart leapt into his mouth when he glanced towards the door. A man with white hair leaned on the doorframe watching them. His weather-beaten face and furrowed brow emphasised his age. He wore a pair of black, well-worn trousers and a waistcoat. Perched on the end of his nose was a pair of bottle-end glasses. His scowl was unfriendly and intimidating.

Will nudged his friend, pointing towards the door. They both stared, shocked by the sudden appearance of this strange man. After what seemed like eons, Adam regained his ability to speak.

'Hello, we were just having a wee look round. I hope you don't mind. Then I hurt my foot.'

The man said nothing, but turned his head towards the now empty cabinet. Then, to their total surprise, he gradually faded away until he disappeared.

'Did you see that,' Adam exclaimed. 'We've got to get out of here, now.'

Will was unable to hide the fact that he was scared out of his wits. He grabbed Adam's arm and pulled his friend onto his good leg. With Will's help, they were soon outside. He gently lowered Adam down onto the grass to rest.

'I'll go and see if I can get help at the gamekeeper's cottage.' Will ran the two hundred metres to the cottage and knocked on the weather-beaten door. There was no reply.

It was getting dark when the gamekeeper's Land Rover finally trundled up the rickety track. After parking outside his home, he walked over to where the boys were sitting. 'Is everything okay?' the gamekeeper enquired, clearly suspicious.

'I think he's broken his ankle,' Will stuttered.

The gamekeeper frowned. 'What exactly are you lads doing up here at this time of the day anyway?'

Adam cleared his throat. 'We were just out on a cycle ride when my wheel hit a rock and I fell off my bike,' he replied, hoping his lie was convincing.

The gamekeeper sighed. 'I suppose we better take a look at it then, hadn't we?' He had a look at Adam's ankle. Black and blue bruises had now appeared, but there seemed to be no further bleeding. 'Well, I'm no medic. Come on, let's get you to the hospital to get checked out.'

The boys and their bikes were loaded into the back of the Land Rover and off they went.

Two hours later, the doctor at Wick hospital confirmed it was just a sprained ankle. 'Keep off it for a few days and you should be fine,' Doctor Sinclair advised.

No sooner had Adam arrived home, than a text from Will popped up on his phone. 'Did the hospital find the stolen quaich?'

Adam chuckled as he tapped out a reply. 'Thanks for asking how the ankle is, and no, they didn't find the quaich. I slipped it into my saddle bag, while we waited for the gamekeeper to return.'

Three days later, curiosity getting the better of him, Adam hobbled to the shed where he kept his bike. As his eyes became accustomed to the dimness, he saw to his horror that his canvas saddlebag appeared to be covered in blood which had congealed and dried in places. Staring at it in disbelief, he suddenly realised he was shivering and that his arms were full of goosebumps. For some reason, his mind flashed back to Dalnawillan Lodge and the strange old man they'd seen. Gingerly, he undid the buckle on the saddlebag and pulled out the quaich. As he held it, it was warmed up rapidly. A strange liquid in the cup suddenly appeared, bubbling and giving off a sulphurous gas. Soon the cup's handles burnt his fingers and he was forced to drop it. Within seconds the shed floor caught alight.

Adam frantically stamped on the flames but was unable to extinguish them. Before long the whole shed was ablaze and filled with black smoke. He pushed on the door but it wouldn't budge. He shoved it as hard as he could but still, it wouldn't shift.

As he drew his terminal breath, he saw the figure of the old man emerge from the smoke. by the time the fire brigade had put the fire out, there was little left of the shed, its contents, or Adam McTaggart. The tragic accident shocked the local community and there was a massive turnout for Will's funeral.

A few months after the funeral, the late Adam McTaggart's father John was doing a bit of gardening when he came across the old quaich where the burnt-out shed had stood. Despite the fire, the intense heat had not been enough to melt the cup. What surprised him was that the quaich was shiny, almost like new and the engraving on the side was still legible. He turned it over in his hands, wondering how it had ended up in his garden. Maybe Adam found it somewhere and brought it home. He wondered whether he should hand it in to the police, but then, would they be suspicious as to how he'd obtained it? He considered handing it into the current Earl of Caithness but again, would that also get him into bother? Perhaps he should just throw it away with the weekly rubbish, but somehow that seemed a crime in itself. After some thought, he decided to try and find out a little more about the quaich before making a decision.

The Nucleus building in Wick that held the Caithness archive was a very modern and very impressive building. He felt sure they would have some information about the twelfth earl and his quaich. The young woman on the reception looked up from her computer and smiled.

'Good morning, how can I help?'

John pulled the quaich out of a Tescos bag and put it on the desk. 'I want to see if you have any information on this quaich. It's well over two hundred years old if that helps.'

She picked it up to read the inscription. Suddenly, the image on her computer screen started to break up. There was a loud bang and all the lights went out. The young woman was shaking as she handed the silver cup back to John. 'I'm sorry sir, but we're obviously having electrical problems. There is a local historian called Morag Sutherland who may be able to help. She lives in Castletown. What she doesn't know about Caithness, isn't worth knowing.'

With her hand shaking, she managed to scribble down Morag Sutherland's address for him.

John gave her a wan smile, picked up the quaich and left the darkened building. Arriving back at his old Citroen Dyane, his heart sank; He had a flat tyre. As he pulled out the spare wheel, it started to rain.

Windy Nook was a single-story, whitewashed cottage at the end of Gunn's Lane. The paint was flaking off the sky-blue front door and windowsills. He parked outside and grabbed the quaich from the passenger seat. The dried bloodstain on the seat made the hairs on his arms stand on end. He stared at the stain in disbelief. Maybe he should have taken the *'throw it out with the rubbish'* option after all. After pressing the doorbell, he waited for what seemed like an age, before the door slowly creaked open.

Standing there was a little, white-haired, old lady with piercing blue eyes. 'I don't buy anything at the door,' she said in a firm voice.

'It's okay; I'm not trying to sell you anything,' John said. 'I'm actually I looking for Morag Sutherland.'

She studied him suspiciously over the top of her half-rimmed glasses. 'I'm Morag and what can I do for you, young man?'

John cleared his throat. 'I am reliably informed by the people at the Caithness archives that you are a bit of a local history buff. Something has come into my possession that you may be able to identify for me. I found it in my garden.' Morag gestured to him. 'Well you'd better come in, laddie.'

He stooped to come inside, hair brushing the top of the doorframe. She led him into a small lounge that looked as if it was straight from the nineteen thirties. Faded wallpaper peeled away from the walls and the carpet was threadbare. Every surface was covered with knick-knacks and books. There were books everywhere including the floor.

She cleared a space on an old leather sofa and gestured that he sit down.

'Now, how about I put the kettle on and we have a nice cup of tea? Then you can tell me what you've come about.' She shuffled out of the room.

Morag struck him as a strange, but friendly kind of woman. He guessed her to be in her late eighties.

They drank the tea, making polite conversation about her interest in Caithness and its extraordinary history.

'I've lived here all my life so I know a fair bit about the county,' she said proudly. 'Now, what is it you have you in that bag?'

As soon as John pulled the quaich out of the bag, Morag gasped in horror. 'Just remind me just where you found it?' she stammered.

'In my back garden, but how it got there is a mystery.

She was glaring at the quaich, as if under some sort of spell.

'Get it out of here,' she said, clearly distressed. 'I'm not having that thing in my house. I'm quite happy to discuss it, but only when it's out of my house.'

Why she was so scared of a silly old cup he couldn't imagine. He took the bag back to his car, before returning, eager to find out what had frightened her so much.

Once she'd calmed down, Morag pulled a book from a pile on her side table. He noticed it had the title, 'Myths and Legends of Caithness.'

She opened the book at page ninety-nine and handed it to him. There was a drawing of the exact quaich he'd found.

'What you have found is an object that's been lost to the world for many years. It's known as the Caithness Quaich and its maker put a curse on it over two hundred years ago. The curse states that anyone who possesses it will be cursed with bad luck. Now you know why I wanted it out of my house. The story goes that the curse can only be broken if the quaich is returned to the family of its rightful owner. It is said that once returned, its rightful owners will be blessed with good fortune for the rest of their lives.'

John had never been one to believe in curses or myths, but had to admit he and his family had suffered a terrible run of bad luck, recently. The horrific death of his beloved son was something he and his wife were still trying to come to terms with.

'So we need to return the quaich to the present Earl of Caithness then,' he replied.

Morag shook her head. 'If only it were that simple,' she sighed. 'It is said that, back in 1784, the twelfth earl refused to pay the silversmith for making the quaich, so he put the curse on the earl, the quaich and anyone who possessed it.'

'What you're saying is that actually the silversmith's family are the rightful owners?'

'Exactly,' Morag replied. 'I've been studying Caithness history for most of my adult life, young man. The whereabouts of the Caithness Quaich has been a mystery for a long, long time. About ten years ago, a family who'd moved up from London found some old papers under the floorboards of their Dunnet cottage. Having discovered that I was a local historian, the young woman thought the documents might be of interest to me. Little did I know that these papers would reveal the name of the silversmith who made the infamous Caithness Quaich. In effect they were a crude set of accounts for silversmith Fergus Mackay. The Caithness Quaich commission appeared in the accounts for December 1784. It shows the debt was never paid.'

John replaced his cup on the matching saucer. 'The question is, where do we go from here?'

Morag hauled herself up from the chair and shuffled over to the window. She stood there for a while looking out into the garden, before turning to face him. 'What is vitally important is that the cursed quaich cannot harm anyone else. For that reason alone, it will have to be hidden somewhere remote, where it cannot be found. Then, if we manage to trace a living descendant of Fergus Mackay we'll be able to return it to them.'

John rubbed his chin in thought. 'That's all very well, but there are a awful lot of Mackays in Caithness.'

She smiled. 'But not that many called Fergus.'

John decided that the best place to hide the dreaded quaich was in one of Caithness's numerous derelict cottages. It would have to be somewhere isolated, to ensure it remained hidden. He settled on an old tumbledown croft near to Westerdale. It could be reached by a rough track that few people knew about.

The narrow tyres of John's Citroen cut through the early morning frost as he made his way down the single-track road toward Westerdale. He crossed the River Thurso, passing the old mill on his right. The waterfall was in full flow after last week's heavy rain. Soon he came to the rough track on the left where he turned off. The car laboured up a short uphill section, bringing him the summit of a small hill. Before him lay beautiful but desolate moorland. The track snaked down the hill into the distance, with the River Thurso to his right. The track terminated at the abandoned cottage. Descending the other side of the hill, the car picked up speed. He pressed his foot gently on the brake to slow his progress, but to his horror nothing happened. He pumped the brake again, but his foot went straight to the floor.

'Oh, my God, what the bloody hells going on now,' he yelled. The car was gaining speed at an alarming rate. He pulled on the hand break, but this didn't achieve much either. With his heart in his mouth he dropped the car down a gear, making the tiny engine scream in defiance. He switched off the ignition to arrest the cars velocity. Finally, as the gradient of the track levelled off, the car spluttered to a halt.

Sweating and heart thumping like a bass drum, he leapt out of the car and headed straight for the boot. After grabbing the Tesco bag in which he'd put the quaich, he marched towards the cottage. The roof had long since gone and the walls were now little higher than a Shetland pony. Wisps of grass grew from crevices in the wall and the floor had gone back to nature. In the corner of the building was a small pile of stone. Finding a suitable low-down gap in the wall, John rammed the plastic bag into it, before piling the stones against it.

The journey to his home in Halkirk was a very slow one, on account of his lack of braking power. On taking the Citroen to his local garage, it transpired that a brake pipe had come adrift.

It was a cold but sunny day as John's little red Citroen pulled up outside Windy Nook cottage. Morag opened the door as he alighted from the car.

She looked excited. 'Come on in, young man, I've got something to show you.'

He followed her into the house, shutting the door behind him. 'In here laddie, I think I may have found a living descendant of Fergus Mackay.'

On the dining table was a laptop. 'I didn't have you down as a computer buff,' he exclaimed.

She gave him a sly look and then smiled. 'We oldies don't just sit around all day.'

'I'm sorry, Morag, it was wrong of me to make assumptions.'

'Never mind all that now, laddie, just take a look at this.'

He sat down and perused the information from an ancestry website. The data showed details for a certain Fergus Mackay. He was born in 1723 and died in 1801, making him seventy-eight years old.

John glanced across to Morag, doubt in his eyes. 'But how can you be sure, this is our man?'

'You scroll down a bit, laddie, and you'll see.'

John read on, spending quite some time, checking and rechecking Morag's work. The website confirmed that Fergus Mackay had been a silversmith who'd lived in Dunnet at the time when the quaich would have been made. It was clear that Morag's research was spot on.

John leaned back on his chair and smiled. 'So it seems Fergus does have a living descendant, named Donald.'

Morag was grinning like the Cheshire cat. 'I told you we oldies were no fools. Donald Mackay's a gamekeeper and lives at Keepers Cottage, Dalnawillan, near Halkirk.' She scribbled his address on the back of an old envelope, which she handed to John. 'Now all you have to do, is deliver that wretched quaich back to its rightful owner.'

The journey across to Dalnawillan was thankfully uneventful and, after some explanation, Donald was happy to take delivery of the old quaich. As John turned to leave, he swore he saw the face of an old man with white hair and bottle-end glasses watching him from an upstairs window of Dalnawillian Lodge.

Meet our authors

Catherine M Byrne
https://www.facebook.com/Cathsbookpage
https://www.amazon.co.uk/gp/product/B07XXC63DQ?ref

Meg Macleod

https://www.amazon.co.uk/Raven-Songs-Meg-

Macleod/dp/0995752109/ref

Shaeon Gunason Pottinger

htpp://tinyurl.com/sharonspage

Jean McLennan

http://www.jeanmclennan.co.uk

Margaret Mackay

https://www.amazon.co.uk/No-More-Secrets-Lies-ebook/dp/B00NHOLIE2/ref=

Printed in Great Britain
by Amazon